T08106

GOODWIN, H.   F(G)

LIBRARY

D0657911

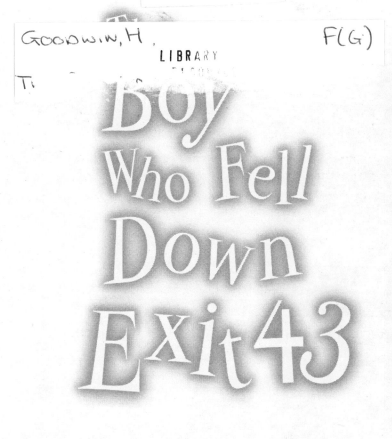

Boy
Who Fell
Down
Exit 43

To
Joseph,
Gabriel,
Harry
and Alfie.

Find out more about Harriet at
www.harrietgoodwinbooks.com

STRIPES PUBLISHING
An imprint of Magi Publications
1 The Coda Centre, 189 Munster Road
London SW6 6AW

A paperback original
First published in Great Britain in 2009

Text copyright © Harriet Goodwin, 2009
Cover copyright © Stripes Publishing Ltd, 2009
Inside illustrations copyright © Richard Allen, 2009

ISBN 978-1-84715-090-5

The right of Harriet Goodwin and Richard Allen to be identified as the
author and illustrator of this work respectively has been asserted by them in
accordance with the Copyright, Designs and Patents Act, 1988.

All rights reserved.

A CIP catalogue record for this book is available from the British Library.

This book is sold subject to the condition that it shall not,
by way of trade or otherwise, be lent, resold, hired out, or otherwise
circulated without the publisher's prior consent
in any form of binding or cover other than that in which it
is published and without a similar condition, including this condition, being
imposed upon the subsequent purchaser.

Printed and bound in the UK.

10 9 8 7 6 5 4 3

The Boy Who Fell Down Exit 43

Stripes

Harriet Goodwin

LIBRARY
RESOURCE
CENTRE

F(G)

TAGGED

I.

Joyride

If he was lucky he'd have about fifty minutes.

And if he wasn't – well, if he wasn't then he'd be in about the biggest trouble imaginable.

It wouldn't actually be a joyride. Not exactly. After all, it was his mum's car, not some total stranger's – and he wasn't out to break the speed limit or try anything too clever.

All he wanted was to get away. Just for a bit. Finn Oliver, twelve years old tomorrow, in command of an old banger for fifty fantastic minutes.

It would be his birthday present to himself. In fact it would probably be his only birthday present. No one else was likely to remember.

Finn glanced out of the window.

If only the rain would stop.

It had been like that for weeks now. Sheet upon sheet of it, tipping down from an angry black sky, day in, day out. There'd been thunder, lightning, flooding – the lot. And still it kept on coming.

The road conditions would be terrible. But at least in the car he'd have time to himself. Almost an hour of not having to think about anyone else. No tiptoeing round the house. No tiptoeing round Mum's complicated feelings.

It was two forty-five. Afternoon rest time. Surely she'd be asleep by now.

He opened the fridge door. Half a carton of milk. Probably a bit off, but it'd have to do. And there was a mug set out by the kettle all ready for him to take up with her pills when he got back. By the time she'd swallowed a couple of those she would've forgotten all about him skiving off school again. They always seemed to calm her down.

Finn reached for the car keys in the fruit bowl and crushed them into the palm of his hand, picturing the exact marks they were making in his flesh.

He would count to twenty. And if it was still silent upstairs when he'd finished counting – if it was completely, utterly quiet – then … well, then maybe he'd do it.

✳   ✳   ✳

Mr Henry Glenridding, Watchman at Exit 43 of the Underworld, was not having a good day.

It looked like he'd been landed with a right bunch of oddballs this afternoon.

As if he didn't have enough to think about, what with the rain battering the Other Side and the dividing membrane growing weaker by the day.

He glanced round the antechamber, its walls glistening with bundles of phosphorescent green algae, and then down the queue of wafting spirits.

If they'd all just keep still for a minute, it'd be a start.

But that was the trouble with ghosts.

Always flitting around as if they had nothing better to do.

Not that you could blame them. Floating was pretty good fun after all. And he was as bad as the rest of them.

"I suppose you think you're being funny, do you?" he snapped, peering through his little round spectacles at a thin man at the head of the queue. "How you can even stay *upright* in that ridiculous footwear is completely beyond me."

"Thought they looked rather smart myself – genuine eleventh century, you know. Got them off a suit of armour down in the Museum of Artefacts."

Glenridding folded his arms across his shimmering burgundy doublet.

"Really! Not exactly twenty-first century fashion, are they? And in any case you're not supposed to borrow stuff from the Museum. Not unless you've checked with me first."

He pointed to a stack of boots and cloaks lying on a low flat rock beside him.

"You need to book the dark stuff if you want to visit the Other Side. Probably an umbrella too, given the weather conditions above ground at the moment. You've got to look *normal*, right? They'd spot you a mile off in that outfit. Exit Ascent Request rejected!"

"But I need to get up to the graveyard and find out when my wife's joining me!"

"Sorry," replied Glenridding, his expression softening. "You'll have to reapply another day. Have a word with Lady Fortescue. She'll advise you on the right sort of disguise."

"But I want to know *now*," persisted the man.

"Your wife will join you down here when her time's up," said Glenridding. "When she's done her Inbetween Time. When she's been dead the full hundred and fifty years. Simple as that. It's the same for all of us, sir. Well, almost all of us…"

A hush descended upon the little antechamber.

The thin man sighed.

"You're talking about those Inflammati whatsits,

I suppose?" he said. "Well, it's all right for some, isn't it? Instant transformation into a heavenly body for the chosen ones, hey? None of this Underworld business for *them* – and none of this absurd Inbetween Time either. You call that fair, do you?"

There was a chorus of sympathetic grunts behind him.

"And just when we think we've heard all the bad news, we're told the Dead have *responsibilities*," the man went on. "Fifty years down the mines when I'm alive and kicking and what's my reward? A stinking pile of duties to the Living, that's what. Not to mention an exam in modern expressions before we're allowed up to the Other Side. I mean, what kind of place *is* this Underworld? A police state? I tell you, it makes me sick."

"You'll soon get used to it," laughed a woman hovering nearby. "Being down here has its plus sides, you know. At least you're finally out of your grave and having a bit of a float-around."

"*You call that a plus side?* Look at us all, for heaven's sake! Nothing but a miserable collection of transparent light particles."

"Pretty nifty light particles, though, aren't we?" said the woman. "After all, we can do exactly what we want … waft through other spirits … treat our friends to a good old-fashioned hug … even pick up solid objects if we like. The world's our oyster!"

"It might be yours," grumbled the man, "but it sure as heck doesn't feel like mine. I don't *enjoy* floating about like some half-demented angel. And nor do I think much of everyone passing through me just when it takes their fancy. It's not on."

"Have you quite finished?" said Glenridding, his right eye twitching behind his spectacles. "Because I've got a job to do here."

The thin man turned his back on the row of assembled ghosts and flounced out of the antechamber into the labyrinth of passageways beyond.

"And what about you?" exclaimed Glenridding, squinting down at a hunched and hairy object now at the front of the queue. "You can't go loping around the Other Side like some Neanderthal caveman, you know."

The hunched and hairy object glared back at the Watchman and grunted.

"Oh, I *see!*" said Glenridding. "You *are* a Neanderthal caveman. Should've guessed. Fourth one I've had to deal with this week. Why don't you do us all a favour and book yourself into a beginners' language class? You'll find it'll help no end. Might even stand a chance of getting past me in a few centuries' time."

A ripple of laughter passed down the line of

spirits and then faded away as Glenridding turned on the little gathering.

"No more time-wasters!" he growled. "I'll have you remember this is *not* a Freak Show. And neither is it a Fancy Dress Party! An Ascent to the Other Side is a very serious business indeed. So pull yourselves together! I've room for only twenty on the ladders!"

He shook his head and sighed to himself.

Sometimes organizing the Dead was enough to try the patience of a saint.

✳   ✳   ✳

It had all been easy in the end. No one had given the boy at the wheel a second glance.

True, Finn had bundled himself up in a huge old navy anorak that had belonged to his dad. And he'd pulled his beanie right down over his forehead. Not much of a disguise by anyone's standards. But it seemed to have been enough.

Now, with The Rose and Eagle on his right and the supermarket coming up on his left, Finn flicked the wipers up to maximum and nudged the accelerator.

He was beginning to trust the car. The protective hug of his dad's anorak filled him with courage. Just a year since the crash and it still smelled of him.

13

LIBRARY RESOURCE CENTRE

Finn swallowed against the rising tide of tightness gripping his throat. It always crept up on him when he was least expecting it.

Don't think about it. Don't think about Dad. Don't even go there…

But it was hard not to. Dad had always been there for him. He'd taught him everything he knew: how to ride a bike, how to swim, even how to rock-climb… That had been brilliant. All that business with the ropes and harnesses and the discipline of working as a team, relying on nobody but each other. Of course it had terrified him senseless at first. But with Dad there, spurring him on, he'd managed higher and trickier climbs than he had ever imagined possible. With Dad at his side he reckoned he could have taken on the whole world.

But best of all was the driving. All those stolen Sundays spent practising on the disused Battersea industrial estate. All those secret afternoons when Mum thought they'd been holed up in some nasty pizza place along with all the other embarrassed kids and their newly-divorced dads.

Well, it hadn't been like that with them. *His* dad had listened. Really listened. Right up until that last, terrible Sunday, he'd gone along with whatever Finn had said he wanted to do.

Which included learning how to drive.

Because when he was driving, Finn could blot out all the bad stuff and concentrate instead on reversing and turning and checking in the back mirror. The thrill of moving up the gears, feeling in tune with the engine … nothing fast, mind. It had been about control. About knowing your vehicle. About looking ahead. About seeing the dangers in good time.

Of course it had made the accident all the more impossible to understand. If his dad had been a great driver, then he had been an especially great pilot. He'd won every amateur light-aircraft award going. Finn had even been up with him once. Huddled together in the cockpit, chasing the clouds.

And then one clear April day – just a year ago tomorrow, and his own eleventh birthday – his dad's plane had simply fallen out of the sky during some dumb practice flight, and Finn had been summoned out of maths and into the headmaster's office.

It had been the end of life as he knew it.

He'd never even said goodbye. Their Sunday meeting just before his birthday had ended in an argument.

Not their usual way of doing things.

But life could be difficult and messy when it wanted.

And that week it had timed it to perfection.

So Finn had added a broken heart to his broken home and found himself heading three hundred miles north to a new house and a new school and a new life.

No more father. Not even on Sundays.

No more father and no more London.

Sometimes he hardly knew which was worse.

✳   ✳   ✳

If a ghost could quake in its boots, then that was exactly what Jessie Sherratt was doing right now.

Nineteen people already through to the Exit Tunnel and only one place left on the ladders.

She didn't really fancy her chances.

At least not with Mr Glenridding in his current mood.

But somehow she *had* to get through this inspection and over on to the Other Side.

She missed her family like mad.

And how she was going to cope hanging around down here on her own while they finished off this stupid Inbetween Time, she had no idea.

OK, so the Dead had to absorb enough heat before they could emerge into the Underworld as fully fledged spirits.

But did it really have to take a hundred and fifty years?

It was a dumb system in her opinion – but then who ever said dying was fair?

Still, if she got up the ladders this afternoon, she could at least make a start. Check out the graveyard and find out how long a wait she actually had. Memorize a few dates and then hold out for the Descent. She could work out the maths later.

"Looks like you've got the disguise right!" came a voice from behind her. "Nice simple cloak and boots. Just what I like to see. And of course black's all the rage nowadays. I expect he'll pass you, no problem."

Jessie wheeled round.

It was Lady Fortescue, wafting towards her in a rush of emerald green skirts.

"Much the safest colour, dear. Always goes down a storm with Henry. Wonderful chap, Mr Glenridding. Real gentleman."

She blushed.

"Do make sure you keep that cloak wrapped round you really snug, though," she went on, adjusting the clasp under Jessie's chin. "We don't want anyone seeing that lovely blue crinoline of yours underneath, do we? And besides, if it's done up properly it'll help keep out the cold once you've transformed. Nasty side effect of turning solid, I'm afraid.

"And such beautiful long hair you've got! So dark

and glossy. Sets off your complexion a treat. Pretty little locket, too. Much nicer than the nonsense people wear these days."

"Nonsense?" echoed Jessie.

"I was up there only the other week. Horrible artificial jewellery. Rings in their noses, some of them."

Jessie's green eyes widened. It certainly didn't sound like the Other Side she had left behind.

"You're a Novice, aren't you?" said Lady Fortescue sympathetically. "When did you emerge?"

"Only a few weeks ago."

"Beaten your mum and dad down here, then…"

Jessie nodded.

"It's why I need to get on to the ladders this afternoon. I want to find out how much longer I've got to wait for them."

Lady Fortescue sighed.

"I know, dear. It's hard. Very hard. I still remember waiting for my beloved sister to join me. Felt like I was holding out for ever."

She gave Jessie's hand an encouraging pat.

"But look on the bright side. You've got through the Exit Exam in record time. Bit of a whizz-kid, I shouldn't wonder."

"It wasn't so difficult," said Jessie, reddening. "Just had to answer a few questions on how they talk these days. Remember some expressions…"

"Very clever, I'm sure!" came a voice behind them. "Now move out of the way, New Girl. I think you'll find that last place on the ladders has got my name on it."

Jessie started as a spirit-boy with long red hair and a bronze helmet swooped past her and began to make for the passageway leading into the Exit Tunnel, his crimson robes flying.

"Oh no, you don't!" said Lady Fortescue, hauling the boy back by the scruff of his neck. "I've told you before, young Morgan Bloodaxe. There'll be no pushing and shoving in Mr Glenridding's queue. *Whoever's* son you might happen to be."

The redhead eyeballed Lady Fortescue.

"*Mr Glenridding's* queue now, is it?" he sneered. "I'll pass that little piece of information on to my father. I'm sure he'll find it very interesting."

"I expect he will," replied Lady Fortescue coolly. "Along with the information you've been queue-jumping again."

The boy turned pale.

"Won't be any need for that," he muttered. "I'll get out of your way, if that's what you want."

"It is," said Lady Fortescue. "Now would you kindly leave this young lady alone so she can make her first Ascent in peace?"

"I guess," said the boy, his dark eyes resting lazily on Jessie. "See you around, New Girl. Enjoy the ride!"

And he floated out of the antechamber, whistling softly to himself.

"Sorry about that," said Lady Fortescue. "I take it you hadn't met before? Very difficult child, that one. Thinks he can get away with murder just because his father's Head of Exit. Causes us no end of bother."

She beamed at Jessie.

"Best of luck then, dear," she said. "Not that you'll need it, I'm sure. You're the perfect candidate for an Ascent."

Jessie smiled back anxiously.

"I wish I felt so confident," she said. "There's loads I don't know."

"You'll pick it all up in a jiffy!" reassured Lady Fortescue. "But do keep your dress well covered up. A lot can happen in a hundred and fifty years – and the crinoline's most definitely *out*."

She glided away, patting her bun into position and smoothing her green skirts.

Jessie looked herself over.

Perhaps she'd be lucky after all.

Perhaps she really did stand a chance of getting up to the Other Side.

It didn't seem so very long ago that she'd been

living there. Hard to believe it had actually been a full century and a half, what with the Inbetween Time and everything. But of course she couldn't remember anything about that.

She remembered the accident, though. Clear as day. The heart-stopping fall and the sudden pain and the roaring blackness pouring towards her. And then nothing.

Nothing till all this.

✳   ✴   ✳

Finn could hear an odd whining sound coming from somewhere inside the engine.

He'd driven past the primary school and the bus station. Now the parish church was coming up on his left. An old lady, hunched against the rain under a cherry-red umbrella, was letting herself through the lychgate into the churchyard, a small dog at her heels.

The village was behind him at last. Only the moor lay ahead, a vast bleakness whipped up by the weather into a watercolour of grey-green flecks and swirls.

He'd trade it in for London any day.

Finn wound down the window a fraction and listened to the whining noise against the drumming of the rain.

Don't like the sound of that. Don't like the sound of that at all.

And now the window wouldn't wind back up –
the mechanism seemed to have jammed.

*This car's falling apart. Just like everything else since
Dad died.*

Finn stabbed at the accelerator with a too-tight,
grubby trainer.

The car skidded in response and the whining
leaped up an octave.

*Better not risk it. Better play safe. I'll find a place to
turn. Mum'll be waking up and needing her tablets soon.*

Finn craned his neck to check in the rear-view
mirror. A pair of hazel eyes stared back at him out of
an anxious, freckled face.

He pushed back a stray wisp of mousy hair.

And then his heart missed a beat.

He had company.

A white van. The first vehicle he'd seen since
leaving the village.

Don't draw attention to yourself. Hopefully it'll overtake.

It was getting harder to change gear smoothly.
The car juddered as he tried to push the gearstick
from fifth into fourth. A scraping sensation vibrated
through his fingers. For a moment or two the car
ground on out of gear through the pelting rain.

Finn wrenched the stick into third.

Don't give up on me, he pleaded. *Not now. Get me
home first.*

Behind him, the driver of the white van hooted his horn and swerved out to overtake.

Finn bent his head over the wheel.

But now the driver was lowering his passenger-side window.

"What d'you think you're doing, kid?" he shouted across at Finn through the gap in his window. "You shouldn't be on the road at your age! And in these conditions, too. Don't you know they've put out a severe weather warning?"

For a moment Finn thought he'd got away with it. The white van passed him and began to speed off at full throttle.

Come on! Get lost, won't you? I've got to turn back. What if Mum can't cope again? What if she's woken up early? What if...?

The van's brake lights had come on ahead.

Finn stiffened in his seat. This didn't look good.

There was only one thing for it.

Closing his ears against the orchestra of excruciating sounds the car was making, he gripped the wheel and jammed his foot down hard on the accelerator.

✳   ✳   ✳

"All set?" demanded a voice beside Jessie, rousing her from her thoughts. "Last one up today. Last one for

23

quite a while, if Bloodaxe gets his way. He's called an emergency meeting in the Red Temple this afternoon. Probably started already actually."

Jessie stared at Glenridding.

"Why? What's wrong?" she asked.

Glenridding's right eye began to twitch.

"It's the membrane," he said. "Still giving us a bit of a headache, I'm afraid. The storms on the Other Side are making it very weak. What with the water pressure from the rain and everything. And now Bloodaxe has got it into his head that we're adding to the problem by carrying on with our Visits. Reckons we should abandon them altogether for the time being."

He shook his head.

"Don't get his logic at all. That membrane's been opening up for us for over a thousand years, no problem. That's what it's *there* for, for heaven's sake. It's the rain that's causing the damage – not us. I'm sure of it. There's no other reasonable explanation."

Jessie frowned.

"I will be safe up there, though, won't I?" she said. "From the rain, I mean?"

"Oh, the rain can't harm you on the Other Side," reassured Glenridding. "Not once you've transformed. Not once you've turned solid. No – it only becomes a problem if it finds its way down here…"

He tailed off, anxiety written all over his face.

"But I'm through to the Exit Tunnel?" pressed Jessie. "You're happy with the disguise?"

Glenridding gave himself a little shake.

"Ecstatic!" he replied, his blue eyes twinkling at Jessie through his spectacles. "Lady Fortescue couldn't have done better herself. Black and boring. Safe as houses. Just need to check you passed the Exit Exam. You've brought your stone with you, I hope?"

"It's here, sir," said Jessie, holding out a small lump of purple crystal. "Amethyst Level."

"Fie!" exclaimed Glenridding. "Methinks thou art a clever wench!"

"Pardon?"

Glenridding flushed.

"Whoops!" he muttered. "There I go again! Lapsing back into sixteenth-century lingo when I'm caught off-guard! I try my hardest, really I do. But it's probably time I enrolled on a language refresher course. Brush up on my modern expressions a bit, you know."

He winked at Jessie.

"All I meant was that I'm very impressed with your Exit Exam result. Don't often get to see an Amethyst Level candidate these days. Now! To business! We've not long left."

Together they glided out of the antechamber and made their way through a short, amber-studded passageway into the Exit Tunnel.

Twenty golden ladders rose up from the floor, reaching into the darkness and illuminating the vast chasm with a soft glow.

"Welcome to the most beautiful Exit under the planet!" announced Glenridding, spreading his arms out wide. "Welcome to Exit 43!"

Jessie goggled at the sight in front of her.

"It's incredible!" she sighed. "It's the most amazing thing I've ever seen!"

"Never ceases to astonish," agreed Glenridding. "Beats all the other Exits hands down. And I've seen a few, I can tell you."

"But where's everyone else?" asked Jessie. "The ones who got through before me?"

"Up there already," said Glenridding. "Waiting for kick-off. If you screw your eyes up really tight you should be able to catch little Charlie Wilberforce disappearing up Ladder Two. See?"

Jessie followed his gaze and was rewarded with a glimpse of dark cloak, which vanished a second later.

"Off to sort out a financial crisis," said Glenridding. "He found a nice piece of antique jewellery in amongst all the plastic rubbish down in the Museum of Artefacts. I told him he could take it up to the Other Side and stick it through the letter box at Meadow View."

"Meadow View?"

"New housing estate at the end of the village. It's where his great–great–great–great–grandson lives. Kevin, I think his name is. Down on his luck at the moment. Charlie thought he might be able to pawn the jewellery and make a bit of cash. Reckoned it was more use to Kevin up there than it was to us lot down here. Kind soul, Charlie. Heart of gold."

He beckoned Jessie over to one of the ladders.

"This one for you, young lady. And don't look so worried! The Ascent's a piece of cake! Hold on when you reach the top of the ladder and wait for the instructions. Once you're up on the Other Side you'll have turned cold and solid. And as for coming back, floating down the Exit Tunnel after a Visit is absolutely no different from floating around the passageways down here."

He peered at his reflection in the gleam of the ladder and smoothed down his hair.

"Nothing to get worked up about at all! Just so long as you believe in yourself, you'll be fine. The heat will do the rest."

"*Believe* in myself?" echoed Jessie. "What d'you mean by that?"

"Exactly what I say," said Glenridding. "You must

believe in your spirit powers. You must never lose faith in yourself."

He smiled at her.

"Watch your back on the Other Side, though, won't you?" he said. "Ours is a difficult Exit."

"Difficult?"

"Too exposed," explained Glenridding. "Just the moor and the village. Nowhere to hide. The villagers think we're traveller types."

"But what if I'm caught?"

"You won't be. Strikes me you're far too sensible to let that happen. Anyway, I can't imagine it'll be very busy up there today, what with the rain and everything. I take it you know what you're looking for?"

"Headstones," said Jessie. "Headstones and dates."

"No problem there, then," said Glenridding. "Usual old story. Just remember an hour's all you're allowed. Make your way back to the top of Exit 43 in plenty of time for the Descent. We don't want you getting trapped over on the Other Side and fading away to nothing, do we now?"

Jessie shook her head, her eyes like saucers.

"And don't forget to catch the end of the meeting in the Red Temple when you get back," said Glenridding. "Promised Bloodaxe I'd be along myself shortly. Shame, though – I'd had such a nice afternoon lined up with Lady Fortescue."

And he wafted away, still muttering to himself…

When Jessie reached the end of the ladder, the Exit Tunnel was already reverberating with a tremendous booming voice.

"EXIT 43! EXIT 43! ALL EXIT ASCENTS TO BE MADE IN THE NEXT TEN SECONDS! KICK AWAY FROM YOUR LADDERS!"

Jessie clung to the top rung.

Kick away? *Kick away?* She hadn't reckoned on this. So she wasn't there yet! The top of the ladder wasn't the top of the Tunnel…

She couldn't let go this high up. She just couldn't.

But it looked like it might be her last chance for some time.

She mustn't chicken out now.

What was it Mr Glenridding had said to her about coming back down?

Just so long as you believe in yourself, you'll be fine. The heat will do the rest.

Well, it looked like she was going to have to heed his advice a little earlier than expected…

There was nothing else for it.

She had to get out to the Other Side.

She had to get that information.

And before she could change her mind, she launched herself backwards off the golden ladder.

29

Nine hundred and eighty-five feet above the top of the ladders – and half a mile to the east – Finn Oliver had just lost control of the car.

He'd managed to get past the white van. That bit hadn't been too much of a problem.

But then the car had started to weave all over the rain-drenched road, resisting every attempt by Finn to steer a straight course.

The van driver followed at a safe distance, hazards blinking.

There was no doubt about it. Finn Oliver had been rumbled. He was up to his neck in it.

What'll they do with me? Where do they put an under-age joyrider? Could they send me to prison?

Finn clung to the wheel, his knuckles white with the effort of holding on.

Rain lashed the windscreen faster than the wipers could flick it away. He could hardly see a thing.

And now the car was veering off-course again, crossing over the catseyes and rattling down the opposite side of the road.

Finn wrestled with the steering wheel – but it was no use.

The car had a mind of its own.

Please don't let anyone come the other way. It doesn't

matter about prison. I'll go if I have to … just don't let me die. Don't let Mum be left alone…

But Finn's luck had run out.

Something was approaching from the other direction.

Just a yellow speck on the horizon at first.

A speck that was hurtling towards Finn at a cool ninety miles an hour.

The driver of the sports car saw the danger too late.

In a fraction of a second Finn's whole world spun out of focus. He was no longer Finn Oliver, the infamous joyrider. He was the epicentre of a force-twelve tornado, rotating away from the road and twisting towards the moor.

Snatches of gorse and heather mingled with fragments of vicious sky as the car ricocheted over the drystone wall at the edge of the road.

Still gripping the steering wheel for all he was worth, Finn traversed the moor in a perfect arc. Shards of glass punctured the air.

For a millionth of a second the car grazed the drenched moorland.

If it had come down on any other patch of ground, Finn would simply have been another statistic. Death by dangerous driving.

But the car hit the surface of the Earth at Exit 43.

It slid through the membrane like a hot knife

through butter, plunging into the darkness and catapulting Finn from its shattered windscreen as it fell.

Above him, the moor closed back over the opening.

And at that moment, though no one yet knew it, the entire future of the Underworld changed course.

2.

Exit 43

"ALL VISITS TO THE OTHER SIDE MUST CEASE WITH IMMEDIATE EFFECT!" bawled Harald Bloodaxe, tossing back his mane of dirty red hair. "Torrential rain continues to weaken the membrane and we cannot afford to make the problem worse than it already is."

The huge Viking warrior paused for effect, his words reverberating around the glittering Red Temple.

"If that membrane ruptures, it'll be nothing less than a deluge down here. Make Noah's Flood look like a puddle. And you all know exactly where the water will head."

The hovering audience cowered under his glare. Even the stalactites hanging from the cathedral-like roof seemed to shudder at his massive voice. Only the

Igneous Fountain thundered on regardless, vomiting out fiery streams of rock in the middle of the lofty red cavern.

"To the Fires, that's where! To the Fires! It'll find its way down like rats in a sewer and quench our precious flames. Do I need to spell it out any more clearly?"

A plump little monk in a brown habit raised his hand.

"I-I know these storms are a dreadful worry, Mr Bloodaxe. A dreadful worry indeed. But I'm afraid I completely fail to see the logic in abandoning our Visits. I truly believe we have nothing whatsoever to do with the weakening of the membrane."

"SHOW ME YOUR EVIDENCE, EDRIC!"

The monk shrugged his shoulders.

"I have no evidence, Mr Bloodaxe. I'm just going by instinct. All I can say is that the membrane has been withstanding our Visits for a whole millennium. It's this constant rainfall that's the new factor. We've never known anything like it."

He sighed.

"I was up at the membrane this morning, by the way. Double-checked the saturation levels. It's still holding up OK, you know. There really is no reason to panic yet."

"THERE IS ABSOLUTELY EVERY REASON TO PANIC!"

returned Bloodaxe. "We can't just waft about waiting for the destruction of the Underworld! We've got to *do* something!"

Edric ran his fingers along the rosary beads that hung around his neck.

"I don't think there's anything we *can* do, Mr Bloodaxe. According to the newspapers these storms are likely to go on for weeks and weeks. We must simply hope and pray the membrane holds."

"HOPE AND PRAY?" roared Bloodaxe. "Is that your solution to everything?"

"Often seems to do the trick," replied the monk. "And it's a definite improvement on the ranting and raving option."

He frowned.

"Of course, if I could just crack the formula for my Magmaplastic Solution, I'd be able to paint it on to the membrane and strengthen it. Then perhaps we'd all feel a bit happier."

"Don't make me laugh!" snorted the Viking. "You've been working on that confounded Solution for weeks now. It's obviously going nowhere."

Edric raised his eyebrows.

"We're not talking quick fixes here, Mr Bloodaxe," he said. "That membrane's a complicated work of art. It's the divide between life and death, after all. I'm hardly going to hit upon a strengthening

35

formula just like that. But I'm convinced I'll get there in the end."

He fixed Bloodaxe with a steely glare.

"And in the meantime we simply have to continue with our Visits to the Other Side. The Living need us. All those hidden jobs we get done for them. All those tiny acts of kindness…"

"TINY ACTS OF KINDNESS?" mocked Bloodaxe, the whites of his eyes flashing. "I can almost hear the violins."

Edric nudged Lady Fortescue, who was floating elegantly at his side.

"Nothing wrong with a bit of human kindness," he muttered in her ear. "That bad-tempered Viking could do with a good dollop of it himself, if you ask me."

"WHAT DID YOU SAY?" thundered Bloodaxe.

"Nothing, nothing, Mr Bloodaxe. Frog in my throat this afternoon, that's all."

Lady Fortescue's lips twitched.

"I was merely pointing out how much our descendants rely on us," went on Edric. "They might not realize it, but they'd be lost without us. And it's not all one way, is it? Take the Novices, for example. Simply desperate to get over to the Other Side and find out how much longer they've got to wait for a reunion with their loved ones. If we vetoed the Ascents that would all have to stop."

Bloodaxe rolled his eyes as a wave of sniffing and whimpering washed through the Red Temple.

"ANSWER ME THIS, THEN!" he hollered, leaning forward on the lectern. "Let's just say for a moment you're right. Let's say we Underworld dwellers really do have nothing to do with the stress on the membrane. It doesn't solve the problem of the rain coming down the Exit every time it opens up for us, does it? That water is bringing down the air temperature in the passageways. I expect it won't be long before we start to lose our shape and colour!"

"But that's pure scaremongering!" gasped Edric. "Such a small amount of water represents no threat to us, Mr Bloodaxe. You must know that! And in any case, it's evaporating very nicely before it reaches the base of the Exit Tunnel."

"EVAPORATING VERY NICELY?"

The sniffing and whimpering now gave way to a murmur of assent among the crowd. The Viking seized his advantage.

"YOU MARK MY WORDS!" he bellowed, the blood-stained axe that hung at his side swinging forward menacingly. "Who knows where all this might end? And that's assuming the membrane doesn't give way first. We must abandon our Visits! We must safeguard our future. Our home... Our territory... Our worldly goods..."

Lady Fortescue suppressed a squeak of indignation.

"*Our worldly goods?*" she whispered to Edric. "Now we're getting closer to the truth! All the things he's stolen from the Other Side, he means. All that gold and silver he's squirrelled away inside the inner vault of the Museum of Artefacts. Let's face it, Edric, that's all Bloodaxe really cares about protecting, isn't it?"

"Too right it is," hissed Edric. "Stuff us lot down here, Lady F. And stuff our descendants on the Other Side, too. That man cares about one thing and one thing only. His priceless Viking treasure. And you know what? I'm not going to put up with it much longer…"

"WOULD YOU CARE TO SHARE YOUR THOUGHTS WITH THE REST OF US?"

Edric met the Viking's gaze head on.

"Not really," he said. "I was merely remarking to Lady Fortescue here that she was looking particularly lovely today…"

He lifted his chin and turned to the assembled masses with outstretched arms.

"I admit we're in a very unsettling position right now," he said. "But I also believe with all my heart that short of a miracle there is absolutely nothing that will change our situation. We can only hope for the best and continue to fulfil our duties on the Other Side."

"And so say all of us," chimed in Lady Fortescue. "I'm with Edric on this one. All this gossiping and worrying is doing no one any good. I was saying as much to Henry only this afternoon…"

"ENOUGH, WOMAN!" cut in Bloodaxe. "STOP WITTERING ON!"

He glanced towards the arched entrance to the Red Temple.

"Where is that fool Glenridding anyway? Quite how we're supposed to discuss this matter properly without the Watchman present is beyond me. He gave me his word he'd be along the second he had supervised the Ascents."

"And I'm sure he's on his way," returned Lady Fortescue stiffly.

As she spoke, a luminous explosion of burgundy doublet swished up the steps and into the cavern.

"*Mr Bloodaxe!*"

There was a short, fierce silence.

"GLENRIDDING!" roared the Viking. "You would dare to interrupt my meeting in such a fashion?"

"I'm sorry, sir. Wouldn't do it in anything less than an emergency, sir. But you see, sir – this *is* an emergency…"

"Emergency, Glenridding?"

Glenridding's face had turned the colour of his doublet. It was a moment or two before he was able to continue.

"It was just after the Ascents, sir. Only a few seconds later, I suppose. I was leaving the Exit Tunnel when I heard this terrible noise behind me, sir. Sort of a tearing, rushing sound. Like – like one of those steam-train things we used to see on the main line above the Exit a hundred or so years back…"

"Spare us the history lesson, Glenridding, and get to the point!"

"Yes, sir. Sorry, sir. I turned back to see what was going on and it was then … it was then…"

"Yes?"

"It was then that I saw it land, sir."

"*Land?*" echoed Bloodaxe. "What do you mean, *land*? It was then that you saw *what* land?"

Glenridding gathered himself against an outburst of eye-twitching.

"A car, sir."

"A *car*?"

"Prithee, sir, methinks it hath appeared to us in a sorry state…"

"LANGUAGE, GLENRIDDING!"

"Yes, sir. Sorry, sir. I mean it's taken a bit of a knocking, sir. What with falling down the Exit Tunnel and everything. But it's still more or less in

40

one piece, sir. Red Ford Fiesta. One litre engine. Nice little set of wheels, actually."

The Viking's monstrous jaw had dropped several inches.

"And you say it's on the floor of the Exit Tunnel?" he spluttered. "Of *our* Exit Tunnel?"

"Yes, sir. But that's not all. A split second later something else came shooting down the Exit Tunnel. To be precise, some*one* else, sir. Didn't see him coming till he was nearly on top of me. Didn't make much noise, you see…"

"Glenridding?"

"It was a child, sir – a boy…"

The atmosphere in the Red Temple positively crackled as Bloodaxe's eyes bore into Glenridding.

"Are you telling me…?"

Glenridding nodded.

"Yes, sir. It's exactly what I'm telling you. A boy has fallen down Exit 43."

✳ ✳ ✳

"You complete lunatic! What d'you think you're playing at? Careering all over the road like that!"

Jessie lay quite still in the driving rain and swivelled her eyes in the direction of the voice. A bolt of pain arched through her body at the tiny muscular movement.

41

The man hurrying towards her stopped abruptly and frowned.

"But you're not… It was a boy I saw – I'm sure it was… And where's the car? What the *hell's* going on?"

Reeling from a double dose of pain and shock, Jessie gawped back.

She had been catapulted up from the ladder into a darkness punctuated by emerald pinpricks of luminous algae, shooting higher and higher towards the mouth of Exit 43.

Then had come the impact. A tremendous force whipping across her chest. A force that had surely smashed into her from the opposite direction. A force that had felt strangely human.

And now here she was on the Other Side, spreadeagled amongst the gorse and heather, pelted by rain and staring into the eyes of a man who looked somewhat less than friendly.

It didn't exactly help that a single skull-and-crossbones earring dangled from his left ear. Jessie could hardly take her eyes off it.

And worse than everything else put together, she was hot.

Burning up.

Exactly the opposite of what Mr Glenridding had told her would happen.

Surely this couldn't be right.

"Well? What've you got to say for yourself? *Were* you driving that car? Because if so I'll have the police on to you quick as a flash."

"No … no…" started Jessie. "I don't know what you're talking about. *Honest.*"

"*Honest,*" mimicked the man. "You don't look very honest to me. Wouldn't trust you further than I could throw you. Never mind – the police'll be here in a minute. And an ambulance too, with any luck. That bloke in the other car's only semi-conscious."

"Has there been an accident?" asked Jessie, prising herself up on to her elbows.

She was solid, at least.

That bit seemed to have worked a treat.

Weird to feel the fullness of her own body again.

Very weird indeed.

"Oh, don't play the innocent with me! At least you must've seen what happened?"

Jessie glanced over at the mangled heap of yellow metal straddling the moor road.

If that was what they called a car, she was glad she'd only ever travelled by horse and cart. It had to be a whole lot safer.

"I didn't see a thing," she mumbled. "I just need to get to the village."

A jet of heat shot through her and she fell back to the ground.

"Another traveller, I suppose," growled the man, looking Jessie up and down. "Too many of your lot about at the moment. Grungy clothes and everything. Always standing around watching us. Don't think we don't notice! I saw some others on the moor shortly after the crash. Off like a shot at the first sign of trouble, of course."

He scowled at Jessie.

"Well, you can just hang on and talk to the police. I expect they'll need a statement from you."

Jessie jumped as a wail of sirens sounded in the distance.

"Talk of the devil," said the man. "You stay put, young lady! I'll be back in a tick."

He turned and strode off through the pouring rain.

Jessie waited until the man had reached the road.

Then she glanced around her.

This was going to take some getting out of…

A drystone wall separated the road from the moor.

She forced herself up on to all fours and began to crawl towards it, weighed down by the stiffness of her solidified crinoline dress under her cloak.

Snatches of conversation drifted towards her.

"And you say there was a collision with another vehicle?"

"Yes, officer. Boy racer weaving all over the road. Knew he was trouble the moment I set eyes on him."

"And where is this other vehicle, sir?"

"That's just it, officer. Doesn't make any sense. Flew over the wall and smashed into the moor and just – well – just *disappeared*."

"Disappeared, sir?"

"Disappeared, officer. One minute it was there and the next it wasn't."

Jessie reached the wall and bore right.

"There's a girl on the moor, officer. Says she didn't see a thing, but she's obviously lying her head off. One of those travellers, officer. I saw some others too, but they've all disappeared…"

"Rather like the other vehicle, then, sir."

"No, no! Not like that at all."

"Been drinking, sir? Serious offence if you're over the limit, you know."

Jessie quickened her pace. There was a dip twenty or so yards away. If she could only get to that…

"Haven't touched a drop, officer. Honest to God, there was another car. Ask the girl, sir. I told her you'd need a word."

"I don't think that'll be necessary, sir. If you'd step this way, please."

"But officer…"

"Come on now, sir. No reason for this to get nasty. Just need you to answer a few questions down at the station."

"You mean you don't believe me about the other driver?"

"Nasty dent in your own van, sir."

"But that happened last week, officer. It wasn't me who caused the crash."

The voices faded as Jessie moved further and further away. She reached the dip in the moor and hauled herself upright, peering over the wall on to the road. As she'd hoped, she was completely hidden from view.

And just a few hundred yards away, crouched at the edge of the bleak moor, was the very thing she had come to see.

The churchyard of St Stephen's.

Her final resting place this side of the membrane.

The place that held all the answers.

And it truly seemed to be beckoning her, pulling her in, commanding her to follow the road ahead.

The heat and the pain were threatening to overwhelm her completely now.

But she would do it. She would force herself to do it. She would find her very own gravestone.

And then, even if it used up every last ounce of her dwindling strength, she would find the names of her parents and brother.

Because if she didn't — if she didn't discover exactly how much longer she had to wait for them all – she thought her heart would surely break with loneliness.

✳   ✳   ✳

Circles of light were swimming under Finn's eyelids.

If this was death, he thought, it wasn't as bad as all that.

Of course, it hurt.

There was no getting away from the icy pain eating away at him.

And what it was going to do to Mum just didn't bear thinking about.

Especially with it being his birthday tomorrow.

His timing was rubbish.

But even so, this dying business definitely wasn't all it was cracked up to be.

After all, he still seemed to be in full possession of his mind.

And that had to count for quite a lot, surely.

He remembered falling down what looked like the start of a tunnel. Though how he'd got there in the first place he hadn't a clue.

Tiny specks of green light had pulsed against the darkness.

A bit like the star show on the London Planetarium trip with school last year.

That was only a couple of weeks before Dad died.

On the Sunday night we stood outside together and picked out the different constellations. It was magic – a sky full to the brim with stars.

Finn pushed the memory to the back of his mind. It could stay where it belonged. It hadn't been their last Sunday together, had it? That day had ended a bit differently. And that was the one that counted.

After the little dots of light had come the cold.

Something had slammed into him as he fell, something travelling the other way, something falling – impossibly – *upwards*. In a split second it had sucked all the warmth from his body.

He had struck the ground at terminal velocity.

The impact must have killed him instantly. Jolted the life from his human frame and smashed him to a pulp.

It was weird, though.

The circles beneath his eyelids were becoming brighter all the time.

And what was more – he could hear voices.

"He's here! Look! Just as I said! Exactly where I left him! Thin as a rake. Bit scruffy, too. Covered in cuts and bruises, of course."

"GET BACK! THE BOY IS MINE TO DEAL WITH!"

"But just look at the car, sir! A real twenty-first century vehicle down in the Underworld! We can put it in the Museum. Should just about get it through the passageways. I can see it there now – the centrepiece of our brand-new exhibition! Beats a pile of boring junk swiped off the village tip any day!"

"I SAID GET BACK!"

A shell of pain exploded inside Finn as he tried to raise his head.

The car! Of course! Must've crashed Mum's car!

"He's moving, sir! I swear I saw him stir! Did you see?"

"CAN'T SEE A THING IN THIS CONFOUNDED EXIT TUNNEL! I NEED SOME PROPER LIGHT! WE MUST GET HIM ACROSS TO THE RED TEMPLE…"

"Hold on a minute, sir! The Descents are coming in. Look! Turning back into their spirit forms beautifully! There are the Ambrose twins safely down already. Been checking up on old Mrs Drury, I believe. And over there! Charlie Wilberforce back from his little trip to the housing estate."

Finn's eyes opened just a fraction.

Hardly more than a whisker.

But enough to see exactly what was going on.

And it was some sight.

There were people floating all around him.

A succession of human shapes, wreathed in black.

Men … women … children … appearing as if from nowhere and gliding down a gigantic black tunnel ringed with golden ladders.

It was beginning to make a horrible kind of sense.

The tunnel. The dark chasm. The weird forms drifting downwards.

He should have guessed sooner. After all, he was hardly going to end up in Heaven after all the things he'd done recently. Nicking the car, for a start. Skiving off school whenever he felt like it. And those last, terrible words he'd spoken to his father. Finn Oliver was no way destined for the Pearly Gates.

"This is Hell, isn't it?" he whispered. "This is Hell I've landed in."

Faces swarmed towards him. Concerned faces. Amazed faces. More and more of them. A riot of anxious expressions.

A huge, red-faced warrior dressed from head to foot in scarlet robes, a bloodied axe at his side … a woman in a bright green dress … a dumpy little monk with a string of beads around his neck … a silver-haired old man wearing a puffy red jacket and tights … and each one nothing but a human shimmer of tiny dazzling light particles.

"Tell me!" he asked again, his voice urgent now. "Tell me! I have to know!"

Silent mouths opened and shut.

For a moment it seemed that no one had an answer for him.

And then somebody hovered out of the shadows.

A red-headed boy in a shining helmet and flowing crimson robes.

A boy with pale lips and dark, dark eyes.

He floated down until his face was just inches from Finn's.

And when at last he spoke, Finn could feel not a flicker of breath behind his words.

"This isn't *Hell*," said the boy contemptuously, his eyes flashing with a strange and luminous darkness. "This is the Underworld. Exit 43 to be precise. You are under the surface of the Earth. You are in the place where the Dead wake up."

3.
The Other Side

Jessie blinked.

The heat-waves were back with a vengeance.

And a face was swimming into view under a bright red umbrella.

"Thank heavens for that!" exclaimed the owner of the umbrella. "For a moment I could have sworn you were dead! Gave me quite a turn!"

Jessie looked up into the eyes of a very old woman. To one side of her a mud-brown terrier bristled on a lead. To the other a mossy headstone jutted up from the ground. Rain spilled from the slate-grey sky.

"I've been that worried, dear. You've been out cold for ages. Hit your head on that gravestone. Had me a bit spooked, if you must know."

"The last headstone," whispered Jessie. "The last one left to check…"

The terrier started to snuffle around her. It licked her face – then backed away, whining.

Jessie turned on her side and started to pick away at the damp covering of moss.

The old lady frowned.

"Ancestor of yours buried here? Must be going back a good while. This is the Victorian section, you know. Are you sure you've got the right gravestone?"

Jessie nodded distractedly. Already she could make out the deep furrows of letters inscribed into the stone.

"Sorry, dear. None of my business. I should know how it is."

She dabbed at the corner of one eye.

"My Ted's buried here, too," she said. "Over there under the yew tree in the new bit. Been gone nearly ten years and I still visit him every single afternoon. Regular as clockwork. Grief's a funny old thing. A funny old thing indeed."

The upper part of the headstone was nearly clear of moss. Jessie began to trace the inscription with a trembling finger.

IN LOVING MEMORY OF JESSICA EMILY SHERRATT
BELOVED DAUGHTER AND SISTER
1848-1859

She lurched forward.

Seeing it written there like that made her feel all shaky.

"Definitely need to get you checked out," insisted the old lady, raising her voice against the steady drumming of the rain. "Don't like the look of you at all. All sweaty and pale. Look like you've seen a ghost…"

She fumbled in her coat pocket.

"I'll try my phone again. Been trying to call an ambulance for ages. Think we must be in what they call a *bad reception area*."

"I'm fine, honestly," cut in Jessie, raising herself up in a show of strength. "I don't need any help, thanks. Just have to read the rest of this headstone, that's all. It's the only place left, you see."

"Strange, though," the old woman wittered on. "Reception must be fine on the moor road. Ambulance went by only a few minutes ago. In a tearing hurry it was. Couple of police cars, too. Must've been an accident up there. You can see the lights flashing in the distance. People treat that road like a blasted race track."

Jessie pulled at the remaining moss. It was just as she'd hoped. There were more words underneath. More words and more numbers. Springing to life under her touch.

EMILY JANE SHERRATT   JOHN FREDERICK SHERRATT

1825-1897   1822-1904

It didn't take a genius to work out what this meant.

An empty sickness began to worm its way up from the pit of Jessie's stomach.

It was too long to wait. Way, way too long.

And there was another inscription. Tucked away towards the base of the headstone. Almost an afterthought.

THOMAS FREDERICK SHERRATT

BELOVED SON AND BROTHER

1847-1915

Jessie crumpled back to the ground.

It was too much to take in. All four of them lying together under the cold earth.

Except they weren't.

Not any more.

Not for nearly three weeks now.

They were one short.

And it didn't feel too great being the odd one out.

Jessie began to recite the dates out loud, willing herself to remember every number and fighting off the blackness that was starting to pour back towards her.

"You hallucinating, dear? I really think I should give that phone another try. Be on the safe side."

"No!" murmured Jessie. "Please, no doctors. Just help me get back to the moor—"

She broke off.

The church bell was chiming above them.

"*What's the time?*"

"Good question, dear. Quarter past four, I make it. Best get you out of all this rain. You'll catch your death…"

"But the Descent!" moaned Jessie. "The Descent! I must've missed it. I'll fade away to nothing!"

"Right! That does it!" snapped the old lady. "You've clearly had a nasty bang on the head. Now, if I just stand over here … yes! I've got a signal at last! Hold on, dear. Everything's going to be all right. We'll have you sorted in no time. Can you tell me your name, please?"

But Jessie didn't answer.

She had been sucked back into the kind darkness where the heat could not touch her.

And she was blissfully unaware of everything…

It wasn't until she was being bundled into the ambulance that it happened.

A gust of wind lifted the hem of her black cloak. Almost immediately it fell back down into position – but by then the old lady had seen all she needed to.

"That child is wearing a crinoline!" she exclaimed, her eyes nearly popping out of her head. "I just knew there was something odd about her. Underneath that ridiculous cloak the girl is wearing a crinoline!"

The paramedic slammed the rear doors shut.

"Whatever you say, love!" he said cheerfully. "We'll be off now! Thanks for all your help!"

The old lady stood gaping at the back of the ambulance as it pulled away.

For several minutes she stood rooted to the spot, oblivious to the worsening rain and to the terrier straining at the lead by her feet.

Then she gave herself a little shake and set off back towards the village, muttering under her breath as she went.

✳ ✳ ✳

"Does that mean my dad's down here?" blurted out Finn.

He couldn't help it. The words just tumbled out of his mouth. There was no stopping them.

The red-headed boy shook his head.

"Not possible," he said. "He died when you were still a kid, right? So special rules apply. He'll have been transformed into an Inflammatus."

"*Into a what?*"

"Into an Inflammatus, of course. It's when—"

"HOLD YOUR TONGUE, MORGAN!" bellowed the massive warrior, hurtling forward. "What are you doing here anyway? Who gave you permission to tag along?"

"I wanted to see for myself, Father. Show some initiative…"

"BAD TIMING, MORGAN! VERY BAD TIMING! GET OUT OF MY WAY!"

"But Father—"

"YOU HEARD ME!"

Finn looked about him uneasily.

"I didn't want to cause any bother or anything," he muttered. "I just wanted to know where my dad was."

The lady in the bright green dress glided out of the crowd and beamed down at Finn.

"Lady Alice Fortescue. At your service. And don't you worry, dear. You're not causing anyone a scrap of bother. As for your father—"

"SHUT UP, FORTESCUE!" roared the warrior. "This boy is my property! And he's coming over to the Red Temple with me this minute."

"I do beg your pardon, Mr Bloodaxe," said Lady Fortescue, staring up the wide shaft of the tunnel and shaking her head gravely. "But shouldn't you be checking out the membrane right now? Bombarded

58

with that amount of flying metal … and after everything you were saying earlier… I really think you should take another look at it."

The warrior's head jerked upwards.

"I'd take good care of the boy while you were up there," went on Lady Fortescue. "I wouldn't, you know, *say* anything to him. I'd just keep guard."

There was a moment's silence while the warrior considered.

"Fine," he snarled at last. "You're in charge for ten minutes, Fortescue. That's all I'll need. And then I want to see the boy over in the Red Temple. Do I make myself clear?"

Lady Fortescue fingered a lethal-looking silver neckpin at the top of her dress.

"Of course, Mr Bloodaxe," she replied coolly. "An opportunity like this doesn't come our way every day, does it now? But first things first – you get on up to that membrane and leave things down here to me."

The warrior eyed her suspiciously, then swung round to face the old gentleman in the puffy red jacket and tights.

"Glenridding!" he barked. "Take the Descents out into the antechamber as soon as I've gone. High time they were all debriefed and out of those ridiculous garments in any case. I'll speak to them myself later on."

And with that he disappeared up the tunnel, a fiery explosion of light particles and temper.

The plump little monk with the beads round his neck let out a noisy sigh.

"Hallelujah!" he exclaimed. "Ten whole minutes' peace and quiet. You're a star, Lady F, a real star. I don't know how you do it."

He glanced down at Finn.

"I'll need to take a look at those cuts and bruises," he said. "Touch of camomile might just do the trick. One or two of them look rather nasty."

Lady Fortescue nodded.

"Fine by me, Edric," she said. "But not right now. I want this time alone with the boy. I reckon I've earned it."

"So you *are* going to talk to him?"

"I'm going to talk to him all right!" replied Lady Fortescue. "But not about You Know What. That's Bloodaxe's job – and he's welcome to it. All I want is to make the poor child feel at home. Introduce him to the Underworld *my* way."

She flapped her hands at the little monk.

"So go on! Scoot! Give Henry a hand with the Descents if you're bored."

The monk stuck out his bottom lip.

"Go *on!*" Lady Fortescue shrieked. "Shift it! Get moving, the lot of you!"

The crowd began to disperse, craning their necks to get one last look at Finn before they wafted out of the huge cavern. As the Descents entered the passageway they threw aside their dark cloaks and boots, and Finn found himself staring instead at a fairytale parade of gowns and robes and tunics. He spotted a small girl in nothing but a lacy nightdress and a young man clad in animal skins.

He blinked and looked back at Lady Fortescue.

"What're they all wearing?" he asked. "They weren't like that a minute ago."

"All back in the clothes they died in, dear," she said cheerfully. "They don't need those silly disguises now that they're back down the Exit Tunnel."

"But what were they doing in disguise in the first place?"

"They've been up the ladders, dear boy," said Lady Fortescue. "They've been up to the Other Side."

"The Other Side?"

"Above ground. Sorry – it's a lot to take on board, I know."

"It's fine," said Finn, his head spinning. "I'm just about keeping up."

Lady Fortescue glanced towards the passageway leading out of the Exit Tunnel.

"They'll be gone in a minute. Then we can have a proper chat."

She waited until the last of the Descents had been ushered out of the cavern. Then she knelt at Finn's side and reached out her hand to him.

Almost immediately she snatched it away again.

"So cold!" she murmured. "So very, very cold…"

It was a moment before she had recovered herself enough to go on.

"How about you tell me your name, dear? Always seems like the best place to start."

Finn glanced down at her hand, which now lay firmly back in her lap. He had not felt it in his. Perhaps that was Rule Number One of being dead. No sensation of touch.

And yet she had plainly felt his hand. She'd said he was cold, hadn't she?

"It's Finn," he replied uneasily. "Finn Oliver. And I want to know what's happened to my dad."

Lady Fortescue nodded.

"Of course, dear. I was just coming to that."

She regarded Finn with kindly brown eyes.

"Your father will have taken a bit of a short cut, Master Oliver. Since he died when you were still a child, he will have transformed into a star. Not just any old star, mind. Certainly not part of your common or garden Orion's Belt or Great Bear or any of that lot."

Finn gaped at her.

"So he's up there in the night sky?" he said.

"In a manner of speaking, dear. The constellation of the Inflammati exists in the Outer Sphere, a galaxy invisible to the mortal eye. You can't see it on the Other Side."

"But you can see it from down here, can you? You can see it from the Underworld?"

"You can indeed," replied Lady Fortescue. "And incredibly beautiful it is, too."

"So I could see these stars myself? Now that I'm down here, I mean."

"Oh yes. I'm quite sure you'll get to see them, dear. Don't think there's much doubt about that. There's a special place, you see, deep in the Underworld, where—"

She broke off, wringing her hands.

"But that really will have to keep for another time. It's not my place to tell you all this."

"All what?"

"Don't press me, Master Oliver. Please don't press me. Sensitive stuff, you see. I'm quite sure Mr Bloodaxe will fill you in later."

"That bad-tempered man who went off up the Exit Tunnel?" said Finn.

Lady Fortescue nodded.

"He's Head of Exit," she said. "Mr Big — and doesn't he just know it. Very nasty piece of work — spent his whole life stealing treasure and burning down houses as far as I can make out. And death hasn't exactly improved matters. You should hear him muttering away to himself when he thinks no one's listening. I'm quite sure he's hatching a plan to set fire to the village on one of his Exit Ascents."

"Nice," muttered Finn. "So what's he doing in charge, then? Can't you just, you know, *overthrow* him? Have a revolution or something?"

Lady Fortescue sighed.

"If only it were that simple," she said. "But I'm afraid it's a long story, Master Oliver. Let's just say we owe Mr Bloodaxe big time. Past favours and all that."

Finn shrugged.

"Whatever," he said. "Anyway, the point is you can't tell me anything till Mr Bloodaxe gets back? Right? Not even about these Inflammati?"

"Oh, I can tell you what they *are*," said Lady Fortescue. "I don't think that's going to land me in any trouble."

She glanced around nevertheless to check that they were still alone.

"An Inflammatus, dear, is the soul of a particular kind of human being. A very special kind of human being. When a parent dies too soon, leaving a child to grow up without them, their soul is released to the heavens. Your dad is up there watching over you. Has been since the second he died. And he'll never stop watching either. He's there for good. And he's there just for you."

"Watching over me?" echoed Finn. He began to rub furiously at the tip of his nose. "Are you sure?"

"Quite, quite sure," said Lady Fortescue. "That is his destiny, you see. He is your very own bright angel, dear boy. He will always be within you and around you."

Finn stared above him into the infinite darkness between the ladders.

For a fraction of a second a long-tightened knot lying deep inside his chest threatened to work itself just a little loose.

Then he lowered his gaze.

"Didn't seem so keen to be around me last time I saw him," he muttered. "Seemed to have his mind on other things."

Lady Fortescue eyed him but said nothing.

"So what about everyone else, then?" Finn went on. "What about all the people who don't become these posh Inflammati things? They get to come down here, do they?"

"They certainly do, Master Oliver," replied Lady Fortescue. "But I'm afraid the rest of us have to hang around for ages before we get a stab at a decent afterlife. Our spirits have to warm up below ground, you see. Need to absorb enough energy from the Fires before they can take flight."

Finn frowned.

"The Fires?" he said. "What are they?"

"The Fires are the very source of our being. They rage at the centre of the Earth and give form and light to every Underworld dweller. Without them we would be nothing but trapped spirits, condemned to eternal darkness."

"And how long d'you all have to wait around before you're warm enough to be released into the Underworld?"

"A hundred and fifty years," replied Lady Fortescue. "It's called the Inbetween Time. Came out of it myself just over twenty years ago."

"But I don't get it," said Finn. "It doesn't make any sense. How can I be down here already? What about *my* Inbetween Time? I mean, I've only just died."

It was Lady Fortescue's turn to look confused.

"Only just died?" she repeated.

Then she let out a peal of laughter that rang around the Exit Tunnel and seemed to weave in and out of the shining golden ladders.

"My dear boy!" she exclaimed. "You *are* in a muddle, aren't you? You haven't *died*, Master Oliver. You're a mortal. A visitor. You're alive!"

Something that felt very much like relief exploded inside Finn.

"I'm alive?" he echoed. "*Alive?* But…"

Already he was trying to struggle to his feet.

"Then I've got to get out of here!" he exclaimed. "I've got to get back to Mum. Stop her from worrying. Stop her from—"

The colour had drained out of Lady Fortescue's face.

"No, no, no!" she squeaked, springing upright and circling Finn in a blur of brilliant green. "You can't go anywhere, Master Oliver. At least not right now. You'll get me into a whole heap of trouble! You've got to stay down here and do as Mr Bloodaxe says. You've got to—"

But Finn had fallen back to the ground.

"Doesn't look like I'm going anywhere fast," he muttered. "My head feels all woozy … and I'm so cold…"

He broke off and stared at Lady Fortescue.

"Tell me this, then," he said. "If I really am alive, how come I survived that fall down the Exit Tunnel?"

"I'm afraid I don't know the answer to that one," replied Lady Fortescue, hovering to a relieved standstill in mid-air. "I expect it'll all come out in the wash, though. Things most often do!"

She leaned in a little closer.

"I probably shouldn't tell you this," she whispered, "but the other really weird thing is that you're not actually supposed to be able to *breathe* down here, Master Oliver. You know, what with you being a real mortal and everything."

"Not be able to *breathe*?"

"Not enough oxygen this far down. Air of a sort, I suppose. But nothing fit to support human life. Otherwise they would've dragged some poor unsuspecting mortal down through the upper passageways years ago to—"

She clapped her hand to her mouth.

"There I go again," she said. "Listen to me and my big mouth! Look, Master Oliver. There's only one thing you need to know right now. You're a miracle child, all right? Our very own Exit 43 miracle child."

Finn moaned as another avalanche of icy pain engulfed him.

"Don't feel much like a miracle child," he muttered. "Feel totally rubbish if you must know."

"I'm sure you do, dear," soothed Lady Fortescue. "And we're all going to do our level best to get you sorted out. But the main thing is that you're down here. We've been waiting such a long time, you see. And now at last it seems our dreams have come true – and what's more, it really couldn't have come at a better moment..."

She stopped short.

Finn's eyelids had closed on his pallid cheeks.

68

"Master Oliver? Finn? I'm losing you. Can you hear me?"

But Finn didn't reply.

"We need to get you over to the Red Temple," muttered Lady Fortescue. "Double quick if I'm not much mistaken. See if the Igneous Fountain can warm you up a touch. I'll go and fetch some help."

She gathered up her skirts and turned to make for the passageway leading from the Exit Tunnel.

But someone was already there – and he was staring straight past her.

"Henry?" said Lady Fortescue. "Whatever's the matter? You're as white as a sheet."

"There were twenty," said Glenridding. "There were definitely twenty. I counted them all up, Alice. Every single one of them."

"Twenty?" repeated Lady Fortescue. "Twenty what? You're not making any sense."

With what looked like a huge effort, Glenridding forced himself to go on.

"There were twenty Ascents today," he croaked. "Full capacity on the ladders. And only nineteen came down. She's still up there. The girl who went up last. She never came down. She's still on the Other Side. "

✳   ✳   ✳

"Clear break of the fifth cervical vertebra," said the senior consultant, pointing to a dark line on the X-ray sheet. "That girl has broken her neck."

Yes, thought Jessie, who could hear every word, *yes, I have. But that was a hundred and fifty years ago and this is now. And from where I'm lying, things look a whole lot worse today than they did back then. Give me a broken neck any day.*

"Then what's she doing propped up in bed over there?" hissed his registrar. "I admit she looks a bit under the weather, but none of this adds up, does it?"

"It most certainly doesn't. No heartbeat, no blood pressure, no output from the brain, no temperature reading … and now an X-ray that shows the girl has sustained an injury from which she couldn't possibly have recovered. I don't like it, Angus. I don't like it one little bit."

Nor do I, screamed Jessie silently. *Get me out of here!*

The registrar leaned in closer.

"Nurse Jackson told me she was wearing the oddest-looking clothes when she came in," he whispered. "Very old-fashioned, apparently – and with a dirty old cloak thrown on top of everything. She refused point-blank to take any of them off. In the end they had to pull a hospital gown over the lot."

The consultant glanced at the clock.

"It's getting late," he said. "Professor Montefiore

will be arriving tomorrow afternoon. Brilliant physician, by all accounts. If *he* can't get to the bottom of this, then no one can. So I suggest we forget about it till then and snatch some sleep."

"You get going," said the registrar. "I'll follow on in a minute. Just want to see if the girl's got everything she needs."

He moved away to sit by Jessie's bedside as the consultant left the room.

"How are you feeling?" he asked, checking her wrist for about the twentieth time, but still not getting even the faintest trace of a pulse. "Nurse Jackson tells me you haven't eaten a thing since you arrived. Aren't you hungry?"

Jessie shook her head and looked away. The heat was surging through her in relentless waves. It was all she could do not to scream out in pain.

And what's more, I'm trapped, she thought, fiddling with her silver locket. *Trapped on the Other Side with the Living.*

The registrar smiled at his patient a little warily.

"Is there anything I can get you before I go? Anything at all?"

"I suppose you could try some opium," said Jessie doubtfully. "They gave it to me once before when I was ill. Seemed to work a treat."

The registrar blinked.

"I'm sorry?" he said.

"Opium," repeated Jessie. "It's a painkiller. Haven't you heard of it? You're a doctor, aren't you?"

"I most certainly am," said the registrar faintly. "But I'm afraid I'm not in the habit of prescribing opium. Gone a bit out of fashion, you see."

He cleared his throat.

"Why don't I put the TV on? Leave you with a bit of company?"

Jessie shrugged. She remembered that word from her Exit Exam. Something to do with moving pictures.

The registrar flicked on the set at the foot of her bed and Jessie started as the strange box sprang into action.

"Keep you amused till Nurse Jackson comes back to turn out the lights," he said, making for the door. "Looks like they're in the middle of a local newsflash."

A small, dark-haired woman gazed out at Jessie from the screen. Black streaks of make-up trickled down her cheeks in little macabre streams.

"Is there a message you'd like us to relay to your son?" suggested the presenter, leaning forward and squeezing the woman's arm. "In case he's out there listening?"

The sad-looking woman stared back with unseeing eyes.

"Just come back," she whispered. "I know it's been really hard lately, Finn, what with your dad and everything. But we'll make it better. We'll get there together. I can't do it without you, though – I love you so much…"

Her pale face crumpled and a list of contact numbers flashed up on to the screen.

Poor woman, thought Jessie, her head a toxic cocktail of heat and nerves. *Poor, unhappy soul. Well, that makes two of us.*

The contact numbers gave way to a full-screen photograph of the missing boy.

"We would ask you to get in touch with the police immediately if you see this child," went on the presenter.

Jessie wrenched her eyes away from the screen.

Getting upset about someone else's mess wasn't going to help anyone.

After all, it wasn't as if it had anything to do with her.

✳   ✳   ✳

"If I've told you once, I've told you a thousand times, Glenridding! No more visits! I've re-examined the membrane and we're not risking it another day!"

"But Edric's been up there too, Mr Bloodaxe,"

73

said Glenridding. "He says the boy and the car have made no difference to it at all. It's as it was before. Weak but holding."

His right eye fluttered like a trapped moth.

"I have to go up and find Jessie Sherratt, sir. She's one of us. We can't just leave her on the Other Side to fade away."

Bloodaxe laughed roughly.

"I think you'll find that's exactly what we're going to do," he said. "I refuse to allow another Ascent tomorrow just because some stupid child has gone missing."

He ran his finger across the blade of his axe.

"That girl took a risk going up to the Other Side today. She must've known perfectly well we were considering suspending our Visits. And it's hardly my fault if she missed the Descent deadline, is it?"

"I never said it was your fault, sir. I was just pointing out that I need to go up and find her, that's all. I'm the Watchman, Mr Bloodaxe. Looking after the Ascents and Descents is my job. And Jessie Sherratt is my responsibility."

Hovering at the entrance to the Red Temple, where she was doing her best to hold back a horde of onlookers, Lady Fortescue looked on approvingly.

"You tell him, Henry!" she muttered. "You tell him good and proper."

Bloodaxe curled his lip at Glenridding.

"Call yourself a Watchman, do you!" he sneered. "Right royal mess-up you've made of it today, haven't you! A Novice stranded on the Other Side and a mortal down here with us. Not bad going, eh?"

"You can hardly complain about the mortal…"

"I AM NOT COMPLAINING ABOUT THE MORTAL!" roared Bloodaxe. "I am merely telling you that a rescue mission to recover the Sherratt girl is out of the question. Even if we leave aside the storms, the Exit area above ground is too dangerous now. Crawling with police since the mortal's car accident, by all accounts. Luckily, they were busy checking out the far side of the moor road at the time of the Descent, so our lot managed to make a run for it. But it's too big a risk to attempt an Ascent tomorrow – the girl's just not worth the trouble."

Lady Fortescue shot the Viking a long-distance look of pure poison.

"Get back!" she hissed at the crowd surging above the rugged steps behind her. "Get back and keep quiet, won't you? I'm trying to hear what they're saying!"

"We've got exactly what we wanted, haven't we?" continued Bloodaxe. "A mortal child down here in the Underworld. And as far as I'm concerned, that's all that matters."

"It is *not* all that matters," said Glenridding. "We have one of our own kind to look out for first. Jessie Sherratt is our number one priority. It's not as if the mortal's even *awake* at the moment. Look at him!"

He pointed over towards the Igneous Fountain where Finn lay pale and motionless.

"The boy's been like that for hours," he went on. "And Edric says he's tried everything on his cuts and grazes and they just won't heal. Not much use to us like that, is he?"

"He's breathing," said Bloodaxe. "Don't know how or why – but that's what counts down here. He'll come round. He has to. That child's not going anywhere till he's done his duty."

"We can't force him," said Glenridding. "We can't *make* him do anything."

"I think you'll find we can."

Glenridding pursed his lips.

His eye had suddenly stopped twitching.

"D'you know something?" he said quietly. "I'm going to do this my way, Bloodaxe. I'm not going to be bossed about by some jumped-up, power-crazy Viking one minute longer."

A curious strangled sound erupted from Bloodaxe's throat.

"Tomorrow afternoon," continued Glenridding, "come Visiting Hour, I'm going up to rescue Jessie

Sherratt. I think you'll find I have more than enough support down here. And I think you'll also find there's absolutely nothing in the world you can do to stop me anyway."

Bloodaxe had turned a nasty shade of puce.

"You'll never find her," he choked. "You don't even know where the girl's got to."

"Then I shall use my brain, Bloodaxe. Start at the graveyard and go from there. Ask around a bit."

"*Ask around a bit?*"

"That's right," said Glenridding. "Ask around. Break a few rules. Because at a time like this, that's what rules are for. If someone doesn't get to that girl soon she'll just disappear into thin air."

"WHICH IS EXACTLY WHAT SHE DESERVES."

"*A pox upon thee, insolent cur!*"

"WATCH YOUR LANGUAGE!"

"Oh, give us a break, Bloodaxe. A fellow can speak his mother tongue once in a while, can't he? And I know perfectly well what we're not supposed to do. Don't go near the general public blahdiblahdiblah … only look after our direct descendants blahdiblahdiblah … keep a low profile blahdiblahdiblah… Well, for your information, Mr Viking, tomorrow will be different. I'll do whatever it takes to fetch that girl back in time. Like I said, I'm the Watchman – and the buck most definitely stops with me."

"HOW DARE YOU ATTEMPT TO UNDERMINE MY AUTHORITY!"

Glenridding shrugged.

"I dare," he said, "because I believe in doing what's right, Bloodaxe. Which is more than can be said for you."

"MEANING…?"

"Meaning simply that your motives in all this leave a lot to be desired. Since the day you got your last piece of Viking treasure stashed away down here, you haven't given a damn about our Visits to the Other Side, have you? You don't care about our descendants – and you don't care about any of us, either. Your only concern is for the safety of your precious treasure."

"IF IT WEREN'T FOR ME THERE WOULD NEVER HAVE BEEN ANY VISITS."

"True enough," replied Glenridding. "It was certainly you who discovered the natural magic of the Exit Hour and started up the Visits to the Other Side. And it was you who got us learning all the up-to-date language so we wouldn't be caught up there. But only so you had *carte blanche* to carry on with your stealing and your burning and all your other nasty Viking habits – and only so you could bring down as much treasure as you could lay your hands on."

"THIS PLACE WAS CHAOS WHEN I GOT DOWN HERE!"

"I'm sure it was," said Glenridding. "From what I understand the Underworld was a floating mass of bored old ghosts in those days. Nothing to do and nowhere to go. You transformed things, Bloodaxe. I don't deny it! But you used your power for violent self-gratification and material gain. It was other people who turned your great plan into something useful. Into something worthwhile that would benefit our descendants."

Lady Fortescue suppressed a cheer and beamed in Glenridding's direction.

"You wonderful man!" she whispered to herself. "I could *hug* you!"

"In short, Mr Bloodaxe," announced Glenridding, "you have the moral fibre of a particularly unwholesome slug. And you're not going to bully us one moment longer. We've all put up with it for far too long."

There was a very long silence.

From the steps of the Red Temple the swarm of spirits watched as Bloodaxe hovered in so close to Glenridding that for a moment their light particles merged and sparked.

When at last he spoke, the Viking's voice was colder than ice.

"Have it your own way then!" he spat. "Have it your own way and to hell with the consequences. You go on up there and get yourself stranded along with the girl."

He regarded Glenridding with slit-like eyes.

"Because by the time you find her there'll be nothing much left of either of you."

4.
Escape

"There you go, Ted," murmured the old lady, struggling to hold her umbrella upright while she stooped to place a tiny bunch of forget-me-nots on the grave in front of her. "See you tomorrow, sweetheart. Usual time. Come rain or shine. Just as I always promised."

She reached out and touched the headstone gently with a bony finger.

"Not that there's much chance of sunshine round here at the moment," she added. "Nothing but rain for days on end. It feels like the end of the world..."

She tailed off, lost in thought.

And then she turned and began to weave her way back through the graveyard, her terrier snuffling at the wet grass.

The old lady was halfway towards the lychgate when she paused.

She eyed the section of older graves over to her left.

It wouldn't hurt, surely?

And it might just help her get the image of that odd child out of her head.

She'd had a dreadful night. No real sleep to speak of. Caught somewhere between dream and fantasy as a procession of faces had drifted through her consciousness.

There'd been Ted, of course, but that was nothing to get worked up about. After all, she lived for her dreams of him.

Then there'd been her own dear grandmother, draped from head to foot in a huge black crinoline and beckoning her in close.

And finally the peculiar green-eyed child from yesterday, crying as if she would never stop.

The faces had grown closer and closer together until they had merged into a confusing whole.

It had hardly been a recipe for a good night's sleep.

The old lady sighed and tugged at the dog's lead.

She'd take a very quick peek and then get home for a nice cup of tea.

The headstone was easy to find – the grass still

flattened from the previous day's little drama and pieces of discarded moss strewn over the ground to one side of the grave.

The old lady screwed up her eyes and read the first inscription.

IN LOVING MEMORY OF JESSICA EMILY SHERRATT
BELOVED DAUGHTER AND SISTER
1848-1859

Jessica, she thought to herself. Jessica Sherratt. Pretty name. Wonder what she was called for short? Jess, maybe? No, that was too modern. Jessie was more likely. Yes, that was nice. Jessie Sherratt. That's what they would've called her.

The old lady peered more closely at the dates and clicked her tongue.

Eleven years old. No age at all. What a terrible waste of life.

Still, she would never have known the loneliness of old age. The pain of losing someone dear and going on alone.

"Excuse me, madam! I wonder whether you might possibly be able to help me?"

The old lady whipped round, holding her umbrella out in front of her like a shield and clutching her handbag to her chest.

A silver-haired gentleman stood just behind her. Rain dripped off the end of his nose and a pair of steamed-up spectacles dangled from one ear. He wore a voluminous black cloak, drawn close around his figure.

"What on earth d'you think you're doing? Creeping up on me like that! Gave me the fright of my life!"

The terrier lunged at the stranger, barking fiercely. The old lady made no attempt to pull it back.

"This churchyard's usually such a nice, quiet place!" she muttered. "Here I am minding my own business. Enjoying my afternoon visit to Ted. Paying my respects. And what do I get? Interruptions, that's what! First that strange child yesterday – and now you! Truffle can bite, by the way."

The man stepped sideways, eyeing the dog, which had retreated, whimpering, to its mistress's more familiar ankles.

"Did you say there was a child here yesterday?" he asked, frantically adjusting his spectacles.

"Certainly was," replied the lady. "And Truffle didn't think much of her, either. Young girl. Eleven or twelve, I'd say. In some kind of fancy dress by the look of it. Not that she was in any fit state to go to a party. I sent her off to hospital in an ambulance. She was in a terrible way."

"Wh-what was wrong?" stammered the man. "Prithee tell me, for pity's sake."

The old lady's eyes bulged.

"Pardon?" she squeaked.

The stranger cleared his throat.

"I mean, er, was she ill?"

"I should say so. Delirious. Quite mad, actually. Talking a lot of utter rubbish. Not unlike your good self, if I might say so."

She sniffed.

"Knocked herself senseless on this headstone right here. Reckon she must've landed up with a bit of concussion. Now, if you don't mind, *sir*, I'd like to get off home. Not my habit to talk to strangers."

She set off back towards the lychgate, her chin held high.

"I'm very sorry," muttered the man, following on behind. "I didn't mean to scare you. Look, if you could just tell me which hospital she was taken to? It'd help no end, madam."

"St Joseph's," said the old woman, staring round at the man. "Cottage hospital at the other end of the village. Number seventy-two bus. It's due in shortly. You know this girl, do you?"

But already he was hurrying past her.

The old lady watched him slip through the lychgate and turn towards the main road.

"What's her name?" she called after the dark-cloaked stranger. "The girl you're looking for. What's that odd child's name?"

"Jessie Sherratt," returned the man absent-mindedly before disappearing from sight. "Her name is Jessie Sherratt."

But he need never have replied.

Because she had guessed the answer before the words were even out of his mouth.

∗   ✳   ∗

Finn was being watched.

It was that red-headed boy again, piercing him with a hard, dark stare as if he would never let him be.

"You awake?" said the boy, gliding over to where Finn was lying.

Finn nodded. Then shuddered as an ice-cold hammer-blow of pain coursed down his spine.

"What's going on?" he said. "How long have I been out of it?"

"Nearly twenty-four hours," replied the boy. "You fainted in the Exit Tunnel and haven't come round since. Bit of a wimp, I reckon."

Finn murmured something to himself.

"Talking to yourself now, are you?" mocked the boy. "First sign of madness, they say."

"Just wishing myself a happy birthday, actually.

I'm twelve today."

The boy sneered at Finn.

"Many happy returns, Mortal Boy," he said. "Not that it's likely you *will* return, of course…"

Finn felt his stomach churn.

This was no good at all. Mum would be beside herself by now. She'd probably got the police scouring the countryside for him. Somehow he had to pull himself together and find a way out of this mess.

He glanced away into the vast space surrounding him.

The Exit Tunnel with its golden ladders had been replaced by a high-vaulted cavern, hung with tiny stalactites and curtains of reddish-brown rock. Dazzling ruby-like crystals studded the walls and just to his right a huge fountain belched out torrents of glowing lava.

"So where've they brought me, then?" he asked.

"Red Temple," replied the boy. "Place where we have all our meetings and stuff. They reckoned you needed a warming dose of the Igneous Fountain. Terrible time they had of it getting you across from the Exit Tunnel. Took ten of them, all taking turns at dragging you through the passageways. Practically faded away with the contact, they said. Never felt such cold."

"Yeah, well, I'm still frozen half to death," said Finn. "This Fountain thing's useless."

The redhead glared at him.

"You should count yourself lucky you've fallen down the only Exit in the Underworld that's *got* a Fountain. And there's nothing wrong with it, idiot. Been jetting away quite happily for thousands and thousands of years, that has. It's you that's useless."

He ogled Finn's tent-like anorak and filthy jeans.

"In a bit of a state all round, really, aren't you?" he sniped, smoothing down his own pristine crimson robes. "Look like you've had a fight with a lawnmower and lost. Haven't you got any decent clothes?"

Finn looked away.

"Things aren't too easy at home right now," he muttered. "Not a lot of money spare. Have to make do, my mum and me."

The boy raised his eyebrows.

"Where's everyone else?" Finn rushed on. "Where's that nice woman I was talking to earlier? Lady Fortescue, wasn't it?"

"That old bat! You don't want to be taking any notice of her. Right old busybody she is. Distant cousin of some boring queen, apparently. Hanging on for a great royal reunion."

"So even famous people are down here, then?"

asked Finn. "Even kings and queens?"

"Uh-huh, even kings and queens. Everyone. The whole of human history. All the way from the cavemen to the very newest Novice."

"All here? All in Exit 43?"

"No, not all in Exit 43! The Underworld's a big place! Thousands of Exits dotted around everywhere."

"And they all connect with ground level, do they? With the Other Side? That's what all that business in the Exit Tunnel was about?"

Morgan looked as if he was about to choke.

"That *business in the Exit Tunnel*," he said, "is natural magic, moron. If we didn't go up the ladders, we'd never become solid on the Other Side, OK? And floating back down the Tunnel afterwards is what turns us into spirits again."

He sniggered.

"Not that it's ladders and tunnels at every Exit. It's a sewer system at Exit 81. Gross, huh? Imagine travelling over to the Other Side and finding yourself covered in—"

"Yeah, yeah," said Finn. "I get the picture."

He pulled a face.

"Do all these Exits join up underground?"

"Course they do," answered the boy. "The Underworld's just one massive rabbit warren, right?

We can zip around wherever we want down here. It only gets complicated when we decide to visit the Other Side."

He yawned.

"Anyway, you were asking where everyone was. The bigwigs pushed off ten minutes ago. Lady High-and-Mighty Fortescue included. Rushed off to the Exit Tunnel to say their farewells to Glenridding."

"Farewells?"

"He's going up the ladders. Off to look for some numbskull New Girl who didn't make it back down yesterday."

"And, er, what exactly was she doing up there?" asked Finn.

"Search me. Checking up on some sad relative of hers, I suppose. Like the rest of the suckers down here."

"Is that what you lot do, then? Keep an eye on your descendants?"

"That's what we're *supposed* to do. Wouldn't catch me wasting my time like that. I use my Visits much more wisely."

"Doing what?"

"Nicking things, mainly. Picking a few locks. Bit of shoplifting, maybe. If I'm feeling lazy I just sift through the village tip. You know the kind of thing."

"Not really," muttered Finn.

"In any case," said the boy, "that's where they've all gone. My dad too, most probably. Or else he'll be down in the Museum of Artefacts guarding his treasure from the plebs. There's loads of them down there right now nosing around that car of yours. Which is just fine by me. Means I get you to myself for a bit."

He attempted a crooked grin.

"I'm Morgan, by the way," he said. "Morgan Bloodaxe."

"Unusual surname," said Finn. "Your dad's Head of Exit, isn't he?"

Morgan nodded and tapped his bronze helmet.

"We're Vikings. Isn't it obvious? We arrived down here together. Died in the same battle. I copped it a few minutes before he did."

"Vikings?" echoed Finn. "But you talk just like me."

"Aha!" said Morgan. "That's the clever bit! Brainchild of my dad, of course. Moment we want to make an Exit Ascent, we have to sit a course and take an exam in modern expressions. It's for protection purposes really, so no one gets suspicious if we have to speak above ground. We're all kitted out down here. Classrooms just along from where we are now. Main Library next to the Exit Tunnel."

"But how d'you *know* how we speak?" said Finn.

"Have you got spies listening in on us or something?"

"Kind of. All the language gets picked up under Exit 38."

"Exit 38?"

"Main Exit under London. There's only a thin gap between the Other Side and the Underworld in that part of the country – and the Exit 38 crowd have driven boreholes up through the rock so they can eavesdrop. Some old woman spends all day listening in on a hairdresser's in West Dulwich."

Finn gave a long sigh.

"Wish I'd landed there instead," he said.

"Got a problem with Exit 43?" said Morgan, bristling. "Fussy, are we?"

"It's not that," returned Finn. "I like London, that's all. Best place on Earth. Where I lived before – well, before…"

"Before your father died?" supplied Morgan coolly.

"Yeah," said Finn. "That's right. Before my dad died."

There was a beat.

"Daddy's boy, were you?"

Finn clenched his teeth.

"Why don't you get lost?" he said. "Reckon I've had enough of you, Morgan Bloodaxe."

Morgan smiled.

"Oh, I don't think you have," he said. "I think you'll find this is just the start of a short but very special friendship."

Finn raised his eyebrows.

"Really?" he said, his voice wreathed in heavy sarcasm. "And what makes you think that, then?"

The redhead leaned in closer.

"Fact of the matter is, Finn Oliver, you're a bit of a catch down here. We've been waiting years for you. Centuries, in fact. Some would even say millennia."

"Waiting for me?"

"That's what I said," said Morgan. "Bet it feels cool to be so famous."

Finn bit his lip.

"You might have arrived in the Underworld by accident," continued Morgan, "but now that you're down here, you're going to do a little job for us. With a helping hand from Yours Truly."

The light from the Igneous Fountain reflected in Finn's wide eyes as he stared back at Morgan.

"Small matter of a prophecy to fulfil," went on Morgan.

"Prophecy?" said Finn. "What prophecy? What are you *talking* about?"

"MY PRIVILEGE, DON'T YOU THINK, YOU GOOD-FOR-NOTHING SCUM?"

Both boys twisted round to see the figure of Harald Bloodaxe framed by the craggy entrance to the Red Temple.

Already he was gliding towards them, his face incandescent with rage.

"He was talking," hissed the huge Viking, "about the ancient Prophecy of the Underworld ... about the supreme challenge down in the Gateway ... about nothing less than the Firepearl itself."

∗　　✳　　∗

Jessie sat bolt upright.

Somebody was at the door, squinting in at her through the little window to her room.

Somebody wreathed in black, pushing a battered pair of spectacles back on to his nose and attempting to smooth down a hurricane of silver hair.

Somebody wonderfully, achingly familiar.

The registrar and senior consultant had followed Jessie's gaze and were now hurrying towards the door.

"Professor Montefiore?" cried the consultant, flinging it open and holding out his hand.

He didn't wait for a reply.

"Honoured to meet you, sir! Thank you so much for coming. We could certainly do with your expert advice, Professor. This girl has us foxed!"

The newcomer gave the consultant the briefest of nods and swept into the room like a gigantic bespectacled bat.

"In which case," he said, his eyes locked with Jessie's, "I think I should like a few minutes by myself with the patient, if that's all right, gentlemen. Would you be so kind as to step outside?"

He winked at Jessie as the two doctors shuffled out into the corridor.

Then he closed the door firmly behind them and pulled down the privacy-blind at the window.

"Nearly missed the bus," said Glenridding, still absorbed in flattening down his hair. "All ended up being a bit of a rush. Don't mind if I sit down for a second, do you?"

He collapsed on the edge of Jessie's bed.

"Zounds, wench!" he sighed. "Am I glad to see you! We've all been completely beside ourselves down the Exit."

Jessie allowed herself a tiny smile.

"Wasn't sure you'd even notice," she murmured. "Thought I might be stranded."

"No chance!" said Glenridding. "Give us some credit, young lady. We're one big happy family down Exit 43. Hardly going to leave you on your own up here to fade away. It wouldn't be fair! It wouldn't be *right*!"

95

He peered at Jessie.

"Not that you *look* like you're about to fade away. Come to think of it, you look rather flushed. Are you feeling all right?"

Jessie shrugged.

It was true – the heat was rising up inside her again. But she wasn't about to make a fuss in front of Mr Glenridding. She needed to get out of here, didn't she? And that was going to require every scrap of her concentration.

"I'm OK," she said. "I'm just a bit hot, that's all."

Glenridding leaned forward and felt her forehead.

"*Just a bit hot!*" he exclaimed. "You're positively on fire, Miss Sherratt! No wonder they rushed you off to hospital. But how very strange. It should be the other way round entirely. I'm like a block of ice myself – better get Edric to take a look at you once we're down the Exit."

He consulted his pocket watch.

"We've less than twenty minutes to get to the membrane," he said, heaving himself up from the bed and making for the large bay window at the end of the room. "We're going to have to climb out of this window and leg it through the rain to the bus stop. Lucky they put you on the ground floor, isn't it? Do you think you're up to a mad dash?"

Jessie nodded.

"I'll do whatever it takes," she said. "Just so long as it means I get back. I need to sort my head out."

"Bad news at the graveyard?"

Jessie sighed.

"Something like that," she said.

Glenridding nodded.

"Always difficult in the first few weeks. And especially tough if you've got a long wait for your nearest and dearest."

He pulled open the window catch.

"Right, young lady! Off with that hospital gown. Quick as you can. Those doctors aren't going to wait outside for ever…"

Five minutes later the two dark figures had boarded the number seventy-two bus outside the hospital gates.

"That'll be two pounds and seventy-five pence," said the bus driver, eyeing Glenridding suspiciously. "Taking your granddaughter up on the moor, are you? Horrible day for it, mate. Rain coming down like cats and dogs."

He watched as the stranger reached into his swirling black cloak for the fares.

"And even worse to come, they say…"

Glenridding handed over a ten-pound note and waited for his change in silence.

"Nasty accident up there yesterday afternoon.

Injured driver in a sports car. Other vehicle missing along with the driver. Only a kid driving it, they reckon…"

But his odd-looking customers had already turned away and were making for the back seat of the bus.

"Where did you get all that modern-day money from?" whispered Jessie when they had sat down. "Did someone *steal* it?"

"Certainly not," hissed Glenridding, as the bus pulled off in the direction of the moor. "We're always picking up loose change from the pavements on our Exit Ascents, Miss Sherratt. And I'll let you into a secret."

He leaned forward conspiratorially.

"We're pretty flush down Exit 43 at the moment. Little club got together recently and pooled all their findings. Bought one of those instant scratchcard whatsits from the shop in the village. Bit of a flutter, you know – and they won fifty pounds, just like that! Anyway, one of them let the whole thing slip as they were landing back down the Exit. And when I agreed to keep shtum, they gave me half the winnings. Thought Bloodaxe might go mental if he found out – probably would've forced them to hand over the lot."

Jessie smiled weakly.

It was getting harder and harder to ignore the

building heat inside her. She felt like a volcano ready to erupt at any moment.

"Can't say we've much use for cash on a regular basis," Glenridding babbled on. "But it came in handy enough today, didn't it? Two bus journeys in the space of fifteen minutes – and here's our stop already. Off you get, Miss Sherratt! Watch that posh frock of yours as you get down. It's nearly time for the Descent."

They stepped off the bus into the torrential rain and Glenridding scoured the moor.

"We're in luck," he said, as the bus drew away from them. "The police have packed up. Bit of a nightmare earlier. Very nearly spotted me after my Ascent. Had to make a run for it. You heard the bus driver saying there'd been an accident up here yesterday, didn't you?"

"I know all about it," murmured Jessie. "I was there just after it happened."

"Suppose you must've been," mused Glenridding. "Didn't happen to see a boy fall down the Exit, by any chance? A boy and a car, that is?"

Jessie gaped at him.

"Never mind, never mind," said Glenridding. "I'll explain it all later."

He seized her hand.

"Come on!" he said. "It's nearly time! Half a minute at most. And don't look so worried! I told you before, the Descent's a very graceful operation. You'll probably enjoy it."

But Jessie's hand was already slipping from his grasp. She sank to the ground, her eyes sliding in and out of focus.

There were twenty seconds left.

Glenridding bent down and scooped her into his arms.

He began to lurch through the hammering rain towards the mouth of the Exit, staggering against the unaccustomed jostle of heavy limbs.

Ten seconds to go.

Five.

The delicate membrane of Exit 43 pulsated in front of him.

Glenridding threw himself at the quivering moorland, cradling Jessie's feverish body to his chest.

And the earth relented.

Swallowed man and girl into its bowels.

And with every passing foot of their Descent, Glenridding sensed that something quite strange and terrible had happened to Jessie Sherratt.

5.
The Prophecy
of the Firepearl

From where he lay at the edge of the Igneous Fountain, Finn felt a shiver snake up his spine.

"But what *is* this Prophecy?" he asked, his eyes darting between the two Vikings. "And what's it got to do with me?"

Harald Bloodaxe glowered down at him.

"Everything," he said. "Absolutely everything. You're here to fulfil the Prophecy of the Firepearl, boy. Who would've thought it, eh? A vile mortal like you, born to save the Underworld from destruction."

He whipped round to face Morgan.

"YOU KNEW IT WAS MY RIGHT TO SPEAK OF THE PROPHECY!"

Morgan stared down at the rocky floor of the Red Temple.

"I'm sorry, Father. I just thought—"

"YOU THOUGHT NOTHING! YOU NEVER STOP TO THINK FOR A MOMENT! NOW GET OUT OF HERE! GET OUT AND LEAVE ME ALONE WITH THE MORTAL!"

"I'll–I'll wait for you down in the Gateway, then, shall I?" stammered Morgan. "I'll wait until you're ready?"

"READY? WHAT DO YOU MEAN, WRETCH?"

"Ready for me to accompany the mortal on his quest, of course," replied Morgan. "Ready for me to help him fulfil the Prophecy of the Firepearl."

Bloodaxe glared at his son.

"AND YOU HONESTLY THOUGHT I'D CHOOSE *YOU* AS THE MORTAL'S COMPANION? OUT OF ALL THE BRATS IN THE UNDERWORLD?"

Morgan's mouth fell open.

"But I'm your only son—"

"YOU'RE NOTHING BUT A WORTHLESS PIECE OF SCUM! NOW GO ON! GET OUT OF MY SIGHT!"

Slowly, Morgan began to edge back towards the cavern entrance.

"FASTER!" roared Bloodaxe.

Finn watched as Morgan shot away through the arch and disappeared down the flight of steps.

"Now listen to me!" spat the huge Viking, rounding on Finn. "Listen to every word I have to say."

He licked his thick lips.

"The Prophecy of the Firepearl, boy, is the very greatest story of the Underworld. It is a tale that has been passed down the generations since time began. And it tells that one day a mortal child will release the Firepearl from its elemental enchantments down in the Gateway and win everlasting protection for the Fires that power the Underworld."

Finn tried to focus his eyes.

The cold was beginning to envelop him, making him feel slow and sleepy.

"I know about the Fires," he murmured. "Lady Fortescue told me about them in the Exit Tunnel. They're the flames that rage at the centre of the Earth. They're what bring the Dead back to life."

Bloodaxe snorted.

"Interfering witch!" he growled. "Knew I couldn't trust her to keep her mouth shut."

Finn stared back at him mutely.

"Rising up from the Fires," the Viking went on, "is a sheer and treacherous cliff. And at the very top of this cliff lies the Gateway, the deepest of the Underworld caverns, reachable only through the passages of Exit 43."

Bloodaxe drew nearer to Finn.

"A gigantic dome of silver flames towers up from the centre of the Gateway. And hidden inside that dome, according to the ancient Prophecy, is the

Firepearl itself, encased in its magical enchantments of fire, water, earth and air."

The Viking's face was now so close to him that Finn could make out its individual light particles.

"Which is where you come in, boy. Because the enchantments that surround the Firepearl are crafted from a magic so powerful that only a mortal possesses the necessary power to breach the dome of fire. No member of the Underworld has ever got through it – though many have tried."

Finn sensed the Viking's words curling around him like wreaths of smoke.

"However," said Bloodaxe, "without immortal protection the mortal would be roasted alive once inside the dome. And so the story goes that he must enter the flames hand in hand with a child of the Underworld. Only then can the quest to release the Firepearl begin."

"And that's what Morgan was on about, was it?" asked Finn groggily. "He thought that you would choose him as this special Underworld child?"

Bloodaxe snorted.

"I'd sooner choose a foul urchin who'd been dragged up from the gutter! I'd sooner choose my own worst enemy…"

The Viking hung over Finn like a giant bird of prey.

"It is in my interests to provide you with only the very finest of companions. Because the Firepearl needs releasing like never before. The membrane that separates us from the Living has become dangerously weak. If it gives way, the rain that is battering the Other Side will come pouring down into the Underworld."

He shuddered.

"Not only will that water extinguish the Fires for ever, drastically cooling the temperatures down here and causing us all to fade away, but it will also wash away everything in its path. Every last piece of my Viking treasure will be lost for eternity."

Bloodaxe bent his head and began to moan softly to himself.

When at last he looked up, his eyes fixed like rivets upon Finn.

"Yet the Prophecy, it would appear, has been true to its word. For just as we begin to dread what lies ahead of us, who do you think should turn up to save the day? A nice juicy mortal, that's who! And what an entrance! Slap bang down Exit 43 straight into our laps."

The Viking smiled to himself, his eyes glittering with a greedy passion.

"Are you ready, boy?" he drawled. "Are you ready to fulfil the Prophecy of the Firepearl?"

Finn swallowed.

"Because there's no getting out of here till you've done your duty. No sneaking off through the upper passageways till that Firepearl has been won, d'you hear?"

"The upper passageways?"

"Your return ticket to the Other Side. Your way out of the Underworld. They lead up to the local graveyard through an empty vault in the Victorian section. No good to us, of course. We rely upon the magic of the Exits. But they'll do nicely for you. Always assuming you do as you're told first, that is."

Finn was battling to keep his eyes open.

It seemed that the Viking's voice was coming from a very long way away.

"Can't stay awake for more than two seconds, can you?" sneered Bloodaxe. "Some hero we've landed ourselves with."

He bared a set of dirty brown teeth at Finn.

"You don't have any choice in this," he hissed. "We've already wasted more than enough time waiting for you to pull yourself together. If you're going to carry on playing dead, then we'll simply have to drag you down to the Gateway. Won't exactly be easy, of course, what with you being so cold. And I'm sure it's not what your father would have wanted. But still…"

Finn felt himself being wrenched from the depths of sleep.

"My father?"

"That's what I said, boy," replied Bloodaxe. "Can't imagine he'd have been too happy knowing his son had to be bullied into saving the immortal Inflammati."

"The Inflammati?" choked Finn, struggling to sit up. "But what've they got to do with anything?"

His eyes widened suddenly.

"Hang on a minute! This Gateway must be what Lady Fortescue was talking about. It's the place where you can see all the special human stars, isn't it?"

The folds of Bloodaxe's face rearranged themselves into a snarling smirk.

"*All the special human stars...*" he echoed. "If you weren't such a revolting runt of a mortal I might almost be touched."

Finn began to suck at the air in noisy gasps, willing it to fill his deflated chest.

"Please! Tell me everything! Tell me exactly what you mean!"

"Nice to hear some manners for a change," said Bloodaxe. "And what I mean, boy, is this. If the Firepearl is not won – and very soon – those precious Inflammati of yours will be lost for ever."

"But you said the Prophecy was about saving

107

the Underworld. You didn't say anything about the Inflammati…"

Bloodaxe shrugged, his long hair glowing redder than ever in the glare of the Igneous Fountain.

"Fire and light – light and fire – they both breathe life back into the Dead. Up in the heavens or down here in the Underworld. And if one dies out, so does the other."

He began to glide away towards the entrance to the Red Temple.

"Have a little think about what I've told you," he called over his shoulder. "I'm off to the Museum to check on my treasure. Left some vile brat in charge while I came up here to deal with you. Wouldn't put it past him to sneak off with a piece of precious Viking gold."

Bloodaxe growled to himself and put on a burst of speed.

"I'll be back sooner than you know it, boy. And then it's down to the Gateway – whether you like it or not."

But his final words were lost on Finn. He had slumped back against the base of the Igneous Fountain, the last vestiges of colour drained from his face.

The cold had taken him to itself.

And his pulse had all but stilled.

* ✳ ✳

"Stop staring, won't you?" snapped Glenridding. "I've got to get this girl into Edric's Chamber and the last thing I need right now is a reception committee!"

He glared at the two young peasant boys who had tailed him from the Exit Tunnel and shook his head disapprovingly at their ragged clothes and dirt-streaked faces. Then he turned away and carried Jessie out of the passageway into a cramped, low-roofed cavern embedded with flint and laced with orange moss. Shelves of bottles lined the walls and the air shimmered with a steamy blue fog of pungent gas.

Edric was hovering over a burnished cauldron in the far corner of the little cavern, his back turned.

"That you, Henry?" he muttered distractedly, poking at the swirling sapphire concoction inside the cauldron. "Been testing the Magmaplastic Solution again with a new combination of ingredients, but I'm still getting nowhere. And just when I thought I was finally on to something, too. I'm seriously worried about that membrane now, if you must know. Didn't want to mention it before, what with your little rescue trip going on – but I checked it out earlier and it's not looking good. Did you find the girl all right? Have you brought her back down?"

"You don't half blather on," said Glenridding, lowering Jessie to the cavern floor. "If you'd just shut up a minute and let me get a word in edgeways, I could explain what's happened."

He unfastened Jessie's cloak from around her shoulders and removed her boots.

"The girl's right here," he went on. "Back to her spirit form, of course, but otherwise in a terrible state. She was burning up over on the Other Side. And it was a nightmare getting her back down. I had to pick her up and carry her over the moor in the end."

Edric glided across from the cauldron and bent over Jessie.

"Well, there's certainly no sign of any fading or blurring round the edges," he said. "In fact I don't think I've ever seen such a brilliantly glowing spirit. Hurts my eyes just to look at her. Whatever this is, it's got nothing to do with being trapped on the Other Side. This is something else – something else entirely."

He frowned.

"Where's Bloodaxe got to?"

"No idea," replied Glenridding. "Watching over the mortal, I expect. Or else checking the membrane again. Won't leave that thing alone for a second."

Edric's round face clouded over.

"Can't say I blame him, actually. The membrane's

reached breaking point, I'm sure of it. Under way too much pressure from those storms."

He sighed.

"The boy's still unconscious in the Red Temple, is he?"

"I suppose so," replied Glenridding. "I haven't been up there since I got back. But I reckon he needs as much of the Igneous Fountain as he can get."

"Well, I've certainly drawn a blank with him," said Edric. "Tried every herb I possess to heal those cuts of his and got absolutely nowhere. Some of them are starting to go septic, I'm afraid."

He scratched his head.

"Just our luck, isn't it? We spend all these years wondering how the Prophecy can possibly be fulfilled, what with mortals not being able to breathe down here. And then when one of them actually survives a tumble of a couple of thousand feet down the Exit Tunnel and manages to inhale our immortal air, he goes and falls asleep on us. It's a real puzzle, Henry."

"Doesn't make much sense to me, either," said Glenridding. "But never mind the boy. What d'you reckon about Miss Sherratt here? I did try and get her to talk once we were down the Exit. But there was no sense to anything she said. Just a lot of confused mumbling."

Silence fell between the two spirits as they looked at Jessie, shielding their eyes from the intensity of her brightness. In the corner of the cavern, the Magmaplastic Solution spat and hissed in its cauldron.

"Can't you use some of those herb things on her?" urged Glenridding. "The ones you prepare for people to take up to their relatives on the Other Side?"

Edric scrabbled around in the pocket of his habit.

"Got a bit of feverfew left," he said doubtfully, pulling out a frilly green herb and holding it between his fingers. "But I've never tried it on us lot before. And anyway, it's really only supposed to cure headaches."

He stuffed the plant back into his pocket.

"Wish I had some lemon balm," he murmured.

"Lemon balm?" said Glenridding. "What's that?"

"Kind of magic elixir. Used it in the monastery to bring down fevers. You never know. It might just do the trick."

"Where can we get it from?"

"It's not the *where*," explained Edric. "It's the *when*. Has to be picked on Midsummer's Eve, you see. And we're weeks away from June."

Glenridding sighed.

"Actually, there was one thing I didn't mention," he said. "Can't imagine it's of any use, but down in the Exit Tunnel the girl was wittering on about something hitting her on the Ascent. Impossible, of course, but that's what she seems to believe…"

"WHAT?" exploded Edric. "She told you WHAT? Why didn't you tell me this before?"

"Didn't think it was, er, exactly relevant."

"Not exactly *relevant*? …What time did the mortal come crashing down the Exit?"

"About t-ten past three," stammered Glenridding. "Just a few moments after the Ascents had gone up, I suppose."

Edric's blue eyes blazed.

"Of *course*!" he exclaimed. "I've been missing the obvious! Too worried about the Magmaplastic Solution to think straight. No *wonder* that boy's so cold … and no *wonder* he survived the fall in the first place … not to mention the fact he can breathe down here…"

Glenridding's face had convulsed into a fit of nervous twitching.

"Who would've thought it?" cried Edric, swooping straight through his friend and whooping for joy. "Simple case of Heat Transfer, Henry! The mortal must be brought over here this second! And Lady F too, if we can find her! She can't miss a moment like this! I'm going to treat you both to an extravaganza of science and magic!"

LIBRARY
RESOURCE
CENTRE

✳   ✳   ✳

Morgan shut his eyes and surrendered himself to the magic of the Gateway.

It was always the same.

The stench of burning.

The taste of soot and smoke and ash on his lips.

The racket of the Fires far below.

And close by, the ancient Firepearl of the Underworld, ensnared in its layers of elemental enchantments.

Wreathed in magic and secrecy.

And just crying out to be released.

Sometimes he felt as if he could stay down here for ever.

It felt like the one place where he belonged.

The one place he was understood.

His father couldn't have meant what he'd said back in the Red Temple, surely.

Not now his dream was within such easy reach.

It stood to reason that he would be the chosen one, the child of the Underworld picked to accompany the mortal on his quest to release the Firepearl.

And yet, as far as his father was concerned, reason no longer seemed to come into it.

Of course, Harald Bloodaxe had always had a vicious temper.

A temper that he vented most generously upon his son.

But recently, what with the trouble over the membrane and everything, his moods had become blacker than ever.

The Head of Exit 43 appeared to be losing his grip.

And with it any sense that he possessed a son at all.

Slowly Morgan opened his eyes.

The protective dome of fire reared up before him, its silvery flames bursting from the ground and forming a perfect, living circle around the hidden Firepearl.

Just once before, many hundreds of years earlier, Morgan had stretched out his fingertips to touch the flame, willing it to react as normal fire and fill his spirit form with extra brilliance.

But instead it had flung him back, stinging him with a pain so fierce that his screams had surely echoed through every passage of the Underworld and caused the earth itself to tremble.

Since then he had kept his distance.

The Prophecy was true to its word.

It would take the magic of a mortal's touch to breach that first and fiery enchantment.

The touch of that sickly little runt gossiping away right now with his father up in the Red Temple.

Master Finn Oliver.

Daddy's boy.

Morgan clenched his fists.

He began to glide silently around the leaping circumference of flames.

What challenges lay inside?

What depths of courage would be needed to conquer the enchanted layers of fire, water, earth and air?

There was so much he could only imagine.

But one question he had solved for himself.

Because it was perfectly clear who must emerge the victor in all this.

Sure, the mortal would have to release the Firepearl in accordance with the words of the Prophecy.

But that prize was immortal property – and Morgan Bloodaxe was going to claim it for himself…

Whatever it took, he would be the child of the Underworld to enter the dome of flames.

He would lie in wait down here in the Gateway until Mortal Boy showed up and drag him through the silvery fire before anyone else got so much as a look in.

Then he would speed through the rest of the enchantments with Daddy's boy at his side, snatch the Firepearl at the very moment of its release and dispose of the true victor over the cliff that led down to the Fires.

Morgan Bloodaxe would emerge triumphant from the Gateway to spin a pretty tale of the mortal's tragic end and revel in every last shred of the glory.

He would be valued at last.

A hero indeed.

And no one need ever know the truth.

✳　✳　✳

Finn was flying.

High above the clouds.

The pain and the cold had disappeared.

And a peculiar lightness had settled on his brain.

It was a moment before he realized he was not alone.

Someone was flying close by.

A dazzling figure, reaching out towards him.

His father...

And there was a voice too, a voice that seemed to be coming from within him.

"But it's my time! My time! That's what you said – every Sunday would be for me! For driving ... or for going climbing ... or for just hanging out together..."

His father stretched his arms out wider.

"And it is for you!" he cried back. "Of course it is! You are my world, Finn. There's nothing else comes close. But I can't pass up an opportunity like this ... can't you see?

117

It's what I've always taught you ... we must follow our hearts ... we must always follow our hearts. And next Sunday I must follow mine..."

Their fingers were nearly touching now.

"So some rubbish air show comes before me?"

"It's not just any old air show, Finn. It's the chance of a lifetime. I'll never get to do this again ... and I'll be with you instead on Tuesday evening for your birthday..."

Finn shrank back, a flicker of heat igniting inside him.

"I don't want you there on my birthday! You and Mum pretending everything's the same when it's not! I want you there on Sunday. I want our special time together."

"But Finn—"

"You promised. You promised..."

"I have to go, Finn."

"I'm coming with you, then!"

His father shook his head sadly.

"You can't," he said. "You can't come where I'm going."

"Then I never want to see you again!" screamed Finn, his voice hoarse and fractured. "D'you hear? I hate you! I never want to see you again!"

His father began to spin away in a haze of blinding brightness and Finn was forced to cover his eyes.

"I'll be there for your birthday!" his father was calling back. "Whatever you say, I'll be there for your birthday!"

And then it was Finn who was spinning away, falling faster and faster – away from the figure and away from all the angry words into an altogether different conversation.

Heat was flooding him now, great waves of it, flowing into his body and warming his blood.

Every atom of his body was springing back to life.

It was going to be all right. He was coming round at long last.

All that stuff about Exits and Tunnels and Prophecies and Firepearls ... the kind Lady Fortescue in her green dress ... the Fountain of molten rock ... the snide boy in the crimson robes ... his vile Viking father ... it had all been a monstrous dream. And he was going to wake up from it any minute now—

"You've done it! He's coming round! Well *done*, Edric! Well *done*! And I was beginning to think he was done for!"

"Thank you, Lady F. Very kind, I'm sure. Simple law of medieval physics. Nothing more, nothing less. I *told* Henry it'd work!"

"And your timing was bang on too! Must've separated their hands at exactly the right moment, because he's still breathing just fine."

"Pulled that one off rather neatly, didn't I? Pure guesswork, of course."

Finn's heart plummeted.

He opened one eye the tiniest crack.

And there they all were.

Lady Fortescue … the silver-haired old man … the fat little monk…

Exactly the same as before, then.

And just when he was feeling so much better, too.

He sighed to himself.

At least that Viking boy and his father seemed to have done a runner.

He could definitely do without them right now.

The scene had changed too. The ruby-studded grandeur of the Red Temple had given way to a dingy cave, lined with springy orange moss and reeking of herbs and chemicals. In one corner stood a gleaming cauldron, a brilliant blue potion dribbling down its sides.

And it was then that he noticed her.

A new face shimmering beside him.

A girl floating a couple of inches off the cavern floor, a green-eyed spirit-girl in a fancy blue dress with long dark hair and a silver locket around her neck. She was very pretty. And she was staring at him, open-mouthed.

Both Finn's eyes snapped open.

"*Master Oliver!*" cried Lady Fortescue, swooping down and enfolding him in an embrace that he could not feel. "Goodness, how you've warmed up! Welcome back! You gave us all such a terrible fright. Thought we'd lost you good and proper! Let me introduce you to the others."

She gestured towards the silver-haired old man.

"Mr Henry Glenridding!" she announced, her cheeks colouring slightly. "Watchman here at Exit 43. Witnessed your fall down the Exit Tunnel. Still recovering from the shock of it all, I think."

Glenridding made Finn a neat bow as Lady Fortescue turned to the girl.

"Miss Jessie Sherratt! Collided with you in the Tunnel and ended up in hospital over on the Other Side for her pains. Without this young lady it seems you wouldn't have survived at all."

Finn and Jessie exchanged confused smiles and then looked away, embarrassed.

"And last but not least, Edric! Healer and scientist extraordinaire. He worked out that something called a Heat Transfer had occurred between the pair of you and has just performed a rather miraculous little reversal here in his Chamber. Isn't that right, Edric?"

The roly-poly monk nodded.

"It certainly is," he said. "You must have hit Miss Sherratt just as she'd transformed and become cold and solid. Somewhere near the top of the Tunnel, I suppose. All that cold will simply have smashed out of her system and into yours, affording you immortal protection."

He beamed at Finn from ear to ear.

"And by the same token, young man, the heat from your own mortal veins must have rocketed into Miss Sherratt, leaving her, well, let's just say a touch on the warm side. Of course, by the time she got back down here and regained her spirit form, she'd taken on board a double whammy of heat. Practically on fire, she was. Anyway, all I had to do was reconnect the pair of you. Put your hands together and wait for nature to work its own great magic."

Finn stared at him, speechless.

"There's one thing I ought to mention, though," went on Edric. "I'm afraid I had no option but to leave a trace of immortal coldness in your system. Took your hand away from Miss Sherratt's just before the process was complete. Means you'll still be able to breathe down here. Means you shouldn't be troubled by such mortal concerns as hunger or thirst while you're with us either. Bit of a task ahead of you, you see…"

Lady Fortescue cleared her throat loudly.

"Give the lad a chance, Edric," she scolded, glaring at the monk. "Master Oliver has just undergone a complicated scientific procedure. It's scarcely the moment to pressurize him with all *that* business. And as I said before in the Exit Tunnel, it really isn't our job to tell him anyway."

Edric bowed his head.

"No, no. Of course not, Lady F. Terribly sorry. Don't know what came over me. I just wanted to reassure the boy that the sliver of coldness in his veins will keep him safe while he's down here. And it won't present him with any difficulties once he gets back to the Other Side either. He won't even know it's there. Gives him the option of a return visit to the Underworld, too – should he be mad enough to want one!"

He winked at Finn, whose eyes looked set to pop out of his head.

"And now that you're all fine and dandy, my potions will work *beautifully* on those cuts and bruises of yours, young man. Got my eye on a couple of real nasties, I can tell you…"

Lady Fortescue silenced him with a wave of her hand.

"Thank you, Edric – enough of the gory details! Everyone, I'd like you to welcome our very own hero, Master Finn Oliver!"

Finn blushed.

"Trust you're feeling a little more human, Master Oliver?" Edric burbled on. "Knocked the worst of that cold out of you, I hope?"

"Thanks," muttered Finn, sitting up and tugging open the zip of his dad's anorak. "I feel loads better. In fact it feels quite warm down here now."

"Does it?" said Edric. "Does it really? I was just thinking how chilly it seems all of a sudden."

He looked around at the others.

"Good grief!" he cried. "What's happening to you all? Henry! Lady F! You're losing your colour! You're fading away at the edges. What in heaven's name…?"

He broke off.

"And that noise … what's that noise? Out in the passageway…"

Everyone strained their ears.

From outside Edric's Chamber there came a low rushing roar.

A noise never before heard in the whole history of the Underworld.

A noise alien to every twist and turn of the heat-filled passageways.

And a noise that could mean only one thing.

Water.

6.
Water

Glenridding stared back at Edric, his eyes wild with fear.

"It's ruptured!" he gasped. "The membrane's gone and ruptured! We're done for!"

Lady Fortescue clapped one hand to her mouth and reached out with the other to steady herself against the wall of Edric's Chamber.

She recoiled almost at once.

"The lighting system's failing!" she cried. "Take a look at all the algae! They're sick! They're dying!"

"Hang the lighting system!" retorted Glenridding, gazing down at the blurred outline of his doublet and tights. "Hang the algae! It's us lot that's bothering me…"

He glanced across at Jessie.

"True, Miss Sherratt doesn't look too bad right now, but it can only be a matter of time... And as for the rest of us, we're disappearing before our very own eyes!"

He raked his fingers through his silver locks.

"The Red Temple!" he exclaimed. "That's it! We've got to get everyone over to the Red Temple. And fast. Before it's too late."

Edric shot him a quizzical look.

"It's the only hope we've got, isn't it?" went on Glenridding impatiently. "It's the highest point in the entire cave system. Higher than this Chamber. Higher even than the Exit Tunnel. It'll be the very last place to fill up with water. And it's got the added advantage of the Igneous Fountain. Might just provide us with a touch of extra warmth."

Lady Fortescue wrung her hands.

"But the temperature, Henry," she whimpered. "The water'll cool the air temperature wherever we are. It's probably extinguished the Fountain already. We're all just going to fade away..."

"Calm thee, dear heart, calm thee!" said Glenridding stoutly. "Chill out, Alice! Remember, I'll be with you every step of the way."

Beside them all Finn had scrambled to his feet.

"Just hang on a minute, won't you?" he said. "Aren't you forgetting something? What about me? What about the Prophecy of the Firepearl? Isn't this exactly the moment you've all been waiting for? The day I get to save the Underworld from destruction?"

The others gawped at him.

Even the tumult of the floodwaters outside the cavern seemed to recede at his words.

"The Prophecy?" spluttered Edric, pawing at the beads of his rosary. "So you knew about it after all … but who told you?"

He whipped round to face Lady Fortescue.

"Lady F! You *didn't…*"

"Mr Bloodaxe told me," cut in Finn. "I woke up for a while in the Red Temple earlier on and he told me it was my duty to fulfil the Prophecy of the Firepearl. Said he'd force me down to the Gateway if I refused to go willingly."

Edric gave the rosary a sharp tug.

"Vicious brute!" he exploded. "But you'll have to forget everything he told you now anyway, young man. It's too late for all that. Our duty is to get you safely back to the Other Side through the upper passageways."

"But—"

"No arguments, Master Oliver!" interrupted Glenridding. "Edric's right. This isn't the moment for crazy acts of heroism."

He peered out of the cavern into the flooded passageway.

"Can't think we've got more than an hour before it gets up to the roof," he said. "But if we're lucky we'll have just about enough energy to float above the water level and herd everyone to the Red Temple."

Glenridding turned to Lady Fortescue.

"Alice, dear, will you deal with the passages around the Exit Tunnel? Evacuate the antechamber if there's anyone around, but don't go near the Tunnel itself. It'll be a nightmare at the source of the flood — a complete nightmare..."

"But what if people are trapped up there?"

"They won't be," said Glenridding, putting his arm around her waist. "The membrane's been making everyone nervous for days now. They'll all have been giving the Tunnel a very wide berth outside of Visiting Hour."

"I'd better take a quick look around the Library and Classrooms, though, hadn't I?" said Lady Fortescue. "Might still be a few Novices hanging about at this time of day."

Glenridding leaned in even closer.

"Good thinking," he said. "And I'll check out the Museum of Artefacts. Bound to have been packed down there today, what with the boy's car arriving from the Exit Tunnel. Just direct everyone you find to the Red Temple and I'll meet you there once I'm through."

"Yes, dear," murmured Lady Fortescue, her eyelashes suddenly all of a-flutter. "Anything you say, dear."

"Edric!" instructed Glenridding. "I'd like you to show Master Oliver to the upper passageways, if you don't mind. We need to get him out of here double quick. *What are you doing, Alice?*"

Lady Fortescue was advancing upon Finn with outstretched arms.

"Leave the boy alone for heaven's sake!" cried Glenridding, shooing her back. "We haven't got time for all that – and in any case, the last thing he needs right now is a stream of teary farewells."

He winked at Finn and returned his attention to Edric.

"Keep an eye out for Bloodaxe, won't you?" he continued. "I wouldn't put it past that Viking tyrant to ambush you on your way up and make off with the mortal in some last minute bid to reach the Gateway."

Edric grunted.

"Just let him try," he said grimly. "Don't you worry, Henry. Leave him to me..."

He broke off.

"But what *about* the Gateway?" he said. "D'you think we should check that far down?"

Glenridding shook his head.

"Way too risky," he replied. "Won't be long before the flood breaks through down there. We'd probably get cut off. Anyone messing about at the Gateway will just have to save their own skin."

Edric nodded his agreement.

"Master Oliver!" he said, turning to Finn. "Wait here for me in my Chamber! I'll have to get myself over to the Igneous Fountain and recharge my spirit if I'm to escort you all the way to the upper passageways. And I'll need to deal with those cuts of yours when I get back too. You can't go tramping through this filthy water till I've sorted those out, that's for sure. Miss Sherratt! Come with me, please! I'm taking you straight over to the Red Temple."

Jessie started at the mention of her name.

Already she was hovering backwards to where the Magmaplastic Solution still fizzled and spat in the corner of Edric's Chamber.

"I'm not coming," she whispered.

Everyone turned to stare at her.

"*Not coming?*" echoed Edric. "What d'you mean, *not coming*?"

Jessie looked back at Edric, her lips trembling.

"I can't, OK. I just can't. I'm staying right here."

✳   ✳   ✳

The fault in the rock scissored the entire stretch of roof above Morgan's head.

A colossal bolt of lightning etched like a curse into the Earth's crust.

An unbroken connection with the Other Side.

And a solid reminder of everything he had lost.

Not far above him Morgan could make out tiny droplets of water clinging like beads to the surface of the rock fault.

It didn't take much to work out what this meant.

It had to be getting really bad above ground for the water to penetrate this far.

He floated down to the rocky floor of the Gateway and focused on the haze of golden stars far above him.

It wasn't every day he risked looking up.

But today, what with a mortal actually down here at last and things looking so dire over on the Other Side, he needed to channel his thoughts.

Remind himself of exactly what he needed to do.

Because this wasn't just about saving the Underworld.

This was about saving himself.

Morgan relaxed his focus and allowed his vision to blur.

Through the giant natural telescope of rock the miracle was already beginning to take shape.

There they all were.

Millions upon millions of tiny gold stars laced across an eternity of darkness.

The ancient constellation of the Inflammati, peppering the Outer Sphere with a scattering of immortal dust.

But which one was she?

And would it make the slightest bit of difference if he knew?

Morgan tore his gaze from the heavens and bowed his head.

It was always this way.

It would be gambling his soul to look any longer.

His mother was as absent to him in death as she had been in life.

Stolen from him before he had even uttered his first cry.

His beginning had been her end.

And never had he been allowed to forget it.

Never could Morgan Bloodaxe make up for that first and most terrible of sins.

Until now.

Because now it was time to show his father what he was made of.

It was time to show the lot of them.

And that little runt Finn Oliver was going to help him every inch of the way.

Finn smiled nervously at Jessie.

"You'll have to go with them in the end, you know," he reasoned. "Edric'll be back for you just as soon as they've put their plan into action and got themselves sorted."

Jessie looked away.

"What is it?" said Finn, frowning. "What's the matter?"

Jessie closed her eyes.

For a moment it seemed she had lost the power of speech itself.

Then she jerked her head towards the cavern entrance, where the water surged only a few feet below the steps.

"That," she whispered, her eyes still clamped shut. "That's what I'm afraid of."

Finn frowned.

"Water?" he said. "You're afraid of water? But of *course* you are. Down here all of you are afraid of it. And it's exactly why you should be getting yourself up to the Red Temple as quickly as possible – while you've still got the chance. While you've still got the *energy*."

Jessie remained frozen against the back wall of Edric's Chamber.

"You just don't understand," she murmured.

Finn sighed.

"Well, why don't you try to explain?"

Jessie opened her eyes.

Then she gave a small shudder.

"I drowned," she said. "That's why I'm afraid of what's out there, OK? I drowned in the river. That's how I died."

There was a long silence, broken only by the bubbling of Edric's blue concoction in the corner of the Chamber and the snarl of the swirling flood in the passageway outside.

At last Finn spoke.

"Was it – was it an accident?"

Jessie nodded.

"I was messing about on a bridge with my brother," she said, shivering at the recollection. "The one near the end of the village. Just above where we are right now, in fact. We'd sneaked off after church and decided to play a game – chucking sticks in the river and watching them come out the other side. I leaned over too far – broke my neck in the fall and got swept away by the current."

Finn swallowed.

"You broke your *neck*?" he echoed.

"That's what they've told me down here," said Jessie, shrugging. "And those doctors were going on about it at the hospital, too. I heard them talking."

Finn's gaze drifted downwards. Immediately his eyes were drawn towards the little silver locket that hung at Jessie's throat. Something about it puzzled him. It seemed almost familiar.

"Don't you know it's rude to stare? There's nothing to see, anyway. All the damage is on the inside."

Finn blushed.

"Sorry," he muttered. "I was just looking at your locket. It reminded me of something."

"Only reminds me of one thing," murmured Jessie, biting her lip. "My family. The one thing I want more than anything else in the whole world. And the one thing I can't have."

"None of them are down here yet, then?" asked Finn.

"Not the ones that matter. I suppose some distant relations must be hanging about somewhere. But not my mum or dad. Not even my grandparents as far as I know. And certainly not my brother."

"Your *brother*?" asked Finn. "Surely you weren't expecting to find *him* here yet?"

Jessie hung her head.

"Not really," she whispered. "But I couldn't help hoping it wouldn't be too long. I know it sounds terrible – but he was my best friend, you see."

"D'you know how much longer you've got to wait for them all?"

"Ages," said Jessie. "It's what I wanted to find out about on the Other Side yesterday afternoon. I went up to the graveyard to discover how much more Inbetween Time they've got left."

"And?" prompted Finn.

"Another forty or fifty years for my parents," sighed Jessie. "And about another sixty for my brother."

She paused.

"So it's not even as if there's anything worth fighting for down here," she said quietly. "It's not even worth trying to save myself."

"But you can't think like that. You can't just give up..."

"You wouldn't understand," snapped Jessie. "You don't know what it feels like to be so lonely."

Finn stared back at her.

"But that's where you're wrong," he said, holding her gaze. "That's where you're so wrong. Because I know exactly what it feels like."

* * *

Inside the Museum of Artefacts pandemonium reigned.

Spirits were streaming out into the passageway, any attempt at good manners forgotten as they blasted through each other, their light particles crackling and sparking.

Below the ceiling of gnarled yellow stalactites a jumble of exhibits lay strewn around the cavern floor, some already floating freely on the rising water and knocking against the sides of the battered old Ford Fiesta.

Glenridding flitted this way and that, rounding up terrified stragglers and hauling them towards the entrance.

"Get out of here!" he yelled at a pale-faced man with a spearhead lodged in his chest. "Go on! Shift it! Get up to the Red Temple!"

"But I'm fading away already!" whimpered the man. "I'll never make it over the water!"

"You'll make it if you really want to!" Glenridding shouted back. "Don't look down at it! Think about the Igneous Fountain! Just *move!*"

He scanned the far end of the long cave, and for a moment his eyes rested on the opening to the inner vault.

He could have sworn he had seen something move just inside it.

A rainbow shimmer, a flash of colour…

Glenridding shook his head crossly.

There was nothing in that vault save for a stash of useless Viking treasure.

And no one was likely to hole themselves up with that, were they?

At least not with all this going on.

Once the water reached the level of the opening, the vault would fill up in mere seconds, spilling its contents on to the watery floor of the Museum and dissolving any spirit form that dared to lurk inside.

It must have been a trick of the light.

He allowed himself a wry smile at the thought of Bloodaxe's prized possessions bobbing away on the muddy floodwaters.

And then he turned and followed the last fleeing spirits out into the passage…

Inside the inner vault Glenridding's trick of the light turned to its captor.

"*Please*, sir! Mr Glenridding's leaving for the Red Temple. Please let me go now! I've done my best for you, sir. Truly I have. Guarded your treasure like you said."

"Get down!" hissed Bloodaxe. "He's not to catch sight of you, Wilberforce! And you're not going anywhere! You're staying right here with me and the treasure!"

Charlie Wilberforce's eyes widened.

"But we've got to get out of here! Both of us, sir! The water's very nearly level with the crevice opening. Another moment or two and it'll be pouring inside!"

"THAT WATER WILL NOT TOUCH MY TREASURE … IT CANNOT … IT MUST NOT!"

But even as he spoke, a trickle of dirty water crept over the edge of the opening and splashed down on to the heap of gold and silver lying at the base of the vault.

Bloodaxe dodged the spray and lunged at his treasure, grabbing a jewel-encrusted sword from the pile.

"What do you make of this, then, Wilberforce?" he mused, turning the sword around in his hands. "A perfect piece of craftsmanship, don't you think?"

His eyes grew misty.

"Highest quality Viking gold. The real thing. What more could anyone wish for?"

"Come *on*, sir!" screamed Charlie. "Look at the water! We haven't a moment to lose! Can't you see?"

Without waiting for a reply, he shot up towards the opening of the vault, ducking the stream of water that was now gushing in.

Bloodaxe scooped up a handful of treasure and followed him.

"Here!" cried Charlie, making for a wooden crate floating close to the crevice opening. "Put your treasure down on this, sir! You'll never manage to carry it up to the Red Temple! We're losing our energy as it is!"

The Viking lurched towards the crate and flung himself on top of it.

"Now follow me!" cried Charlie. "Leave your treasure there and follow me to the Red Temple!"

Bloodaxe crouched upon the crate and clutched his treasure to his chest.

"Leave it?" he whimpered. "Leave my precious Viking gold and silver? But it's all I have left. It's all that matters."

Charlie gaped at the Head of Exit.

He opened his mouth to argue – then shut it again and gave a tiny shrug.

"I have to go now, sir," he said quietly. "I have to get up to the Red Temple before it's too late."

He turned and began to hover towards the entrance to the Museum.

And behind him, perched on his little wooden raft, Bloodaxe rocked from side to side and hugged his treasure tight.

＊　＊　＊

Even above the roar of the Fires, Morgan could hear it coming.

He darted towards the entrance of the Gateway and up the narrow staircase leading back into the passageway.

The noise was gathering pace.

A booming snarl, thundering through the tunnels just above his head.

Morgan's gaze swept the entire stretch of passage. But he could hardly see a thing.

He reached out his hand and trailed his fingers over the passage wall.

Gone were the bright and beautiful swathes of iridescent algae, the glittering blues and greens and reds and yellows.

The jewel-like lustre of the Underworld had all but drained away, leaving nothing but a seeping curtain of dimly-pulsating slime.

He imagined how it would be.

The smash of the flood as it swept him up in its relentless path.

The moment of obliteration as he disappeared into nothingness.

The very final death.

There was only one way to turn, and that was back the way he had just come.

He would race that ravenous water down the steps and into the Gateway if it was the last thing he ever did.

And then it was upon him.

A wall of water rounding the final corner of the darkened passageway...

7.
Blood

"I've felt lonely since the day my dad died," said Finn. "He was killed in a plane accident this time last year. Exactly this time last year. It happened on my birthday, just to be sure I never forget."

"It's your birthday today?"

Finn nodded.

"Apparently," he said. "Doesn't much feel like it, though. Not with all this going on. Maybe one day I'll have a normal birthday again like everyone else."

He sighed.

"Guess it wouldn't have been much of a celebration if I'd been at home anyway. Mum never even asked me what I wanted this year. Probably hoped the day would just disappear."

"It must be hard for her as well," said Jessie.

"Your dad – her husband…"

"But he wasn't," said Finn. "That's the whole point. They'd been divorced six months. That's adults for you, though, isn't it? Never make a lot of sense."

"*Divorced?*" echoed Jessie.

Finn shrugged.

"It happens to loads of people these days," he said. "Half the kids in my class come from broken homes."

Jessie gaped at him.

"Was it really terrible?" she asked.

"What?" said Finn. "The divorce or my dad dying?"

His words hung between them in the gloom of Edric's Chamber.

Jessie didn't reply.

"Not much to choose between them, really," said Finn bitterly. "Everything's just a huge great mess. Let's just say you haven't got the monopoly on feeling rubbish, Jessie Sherratt. I feel lonely all the time, OK? Every morning I wake up and for a second I think everything's just as it was. And then it all comes flooding back … that day in maths … this time last year … my eleventh birthday…"

"Go on…"

Finn sank down on to the rocky floor of Edric's Chamber and hugged his knees to his chest.

"We'd just sat down to a test," he said. "It was completely impossible. New stuff we'd been doing

143

the term before – algebra, mainly – and there was a knock at the door and the headmaster's secretary came in. She whispered something to the maths teacher and I got called out. And d'you know what?"

Jessie shook her head.

"I remember thinking, *Lucky me – now I'll get out of the test.* I even put my thumbs up under the desk to my best mate. I mean, how stupid was that?"

"But you weren't to know."

Finn ignored her.

"The secretary took me into the headmaster's office and my mum was sitting there crying. All red and white and blotchy. And I just thought, *That can't be right … Mum blubbing away in front of Mr Mackenzie … and anyway she should be in town … at work…*"

He shut his eyes.

"And then Mr Mackenzie was reaching forward and taking my hand. That's when I knew something was really wrong. Really, really wrong. He didn't hang about. Just came right out with it. *I'm afraid I have some bad news for you, Finn. Your father has been killed in an aircraft accident. I'm so very sorry.*"

Jessie bent her head.

"He'd been out on a practice flight," said Finn. "Flying light aircraft was his hobby, you see. He was crazy about it."

He opened his eyes and gazed across at Edric's

cauldron until his vision began to blur.

Then he looked away abruptly.

"Anyway, I don't remember much after that. The rest of the day just went by in a kind of fog. Phone calls. Kind neighbours. Endless cups of tea for my mother. Not that she drank any of them."

Finn bit his lip.

"My world just split apart that day. Nothing can ever be the same again. And nothing can ever be all right again, either."

There was a long silence.

"At least you've still got your mum," said Jessie at last. "I bet you're missing her like anything."

"S'pose," muttered Finn. "It's a bit complicated, really. She's been on tablets since Dad died. She's always crying and stuff."

Jessie nodded.

"She looked pretty upset when I saw her in the hospital."

"*You saw my mum in the hospital?* What? Are you sure?"

"It must've been your mum. She definitely said your name. And they showed a picture of you, too. She was in one of those box things with moving pictures – what d'you call it again?"

"On *television*?" choked Finn. "My mum was on *television*?"

"*That's* the word!"

"But what was my mum doing on TV? What was she saying?"

"Asking you to come back, of course."

Finn swallowed hard. He leaned forward and began to unlace his trainers.

"Did – did she say anything else?"

"She said she couldn't do without you," remembered Jessie. "She said it'd turn out all right in the end."

Finn's fingers shook as he fumbled with the laces.

"Oh yes," added Jessie. "And there was one other thing. She said that she loved you."

* ✳ *

Morgan clung to the narrow shelf and gaped at the scene as it unfolded beneath him in the Gateway.

Torrents of water cascaded down the entrance steps, crashing against the walls and spewing fountains of spray high into the air.

The floods had well and truly penetrated the Underworld, dashing every one of his hopes and dreams.

The Firepearl would never be released now.

And Morgan's only consolation was that if the glory was not to belong to him, then at least it would belong to no one.

As he had swooped down the rocky stairway pursued by the floodwaters, a shower of spray had caught him unawares and robbed him instantly of his floating powers. He had been forced to scale his way up the back wall of the Gateway to the safety of the ledge.

Now he watched as the flood flared out at the foot of the stairway, devouring the cave floor in a sea of frothing spume and then gathering momentum as it surged ever onward.

At the far end of the Gateway lay the cliff leading down to the Fires.

And between the flood and the edge of oblivion nestled the Firepearl, concealed within its charmed dome of silvery flames.

Morgan looked on as the angry water drew closer and closer to the fiery dome.

It was almost too much to bear.

All that promise.

All that dark and secret power about to be washed away in the churning flood – the mystery of the Firepearl lost for ever.

The moment came all too soon.

The water connected with the enchanted flames...

And from his vantage point Morgan gasped as the shooting tongues of silver fire laughed in the face of nature and flung back the flood with a raw and careless magic.

So the Firepearl would belong not even to the floods themselves. It would remain inside its cocoon for ever, safe but utterly useless.

The hurrying water arched away from the flames, fanning out in two identical streams that joined back up at the opposite side of the circle.

Clear of its obstacle, it continued on its journey.

On and on to the very end of the Gateway.

Over the cliff and down, down into the Fires below.

A venomous spitting rose up from the depths of the Earth.

Morgan craned his neck to get a clearer view and swayed just a fraction on the shelf.

The next minute he was lurching forward, a fading figure flailing and twisting in the growing darkness.

For a split second he clawed at nothing but the rapidly cooling air.

This time the flood would surely have him.

Or else he would be pierced by the flames and meet his end in their mocking jaws.

Either way, Morgan Bloodaxe had it coming.

And then his right hand plunged into a clammy patch of overhanging algae.

He grasped at it like a drowning man, pulling and

tearing at the curtain of rotting slime until, bit by bit, he regained his trembling balance.

Morgan crouched back on the narrow strip of rock.

He reached behind him for another steadying fistful of algae.

But it had gone.

Every last strand had been ripped from the surrounding wall – and in its place there was nothing but space.

Morgan's fingers probed the emptiness behind the ledge.

The emptiness became a hole – and the hole stretched back into a narrow, dry passage, hidden for centuries behind a thick tapestry of ancient algae.

To Morgan it meant just one thing.

The chance of escape.

He feasted his eyes one more time on the battle of fire and water that raged below him.

And then he turned his back on the furious elements and began to drag himself along the secret tunnel.

✳ ✳ ✳

"You're right, of course," said Finn, re-lacing his trainers and standing back up at last. "I've still got my mum. And she needs me back home."

He sighed.

"It's just there's something I would've liked to have done first."

"You're not banging on about that Firepearl again, are you?" said Jessie. "Forget it, Finn. The passageway leading down to the Gateway will have flooded by now. And you can take it from me, drowning is not a nice way to die."

Her fingers reached for the comfort of her silver locket.

"Hang on a minute!" cried Finn, peering at the engraving on its shimmering casing. "That's the crest of The Rose and Eagle! I *knew* there was something familiar about that locket! But what's The Rose and Eagle got to do with *you*? Surely it wasn't there when you were alive?"

"What're you talking about?" said Jessie. "What's The Rose and Eagle? This is our family emblem..."

"Your family emblem? But it can't be! It's *our* family emblem! And The Rose and Eagle's my aunt's pub! It's been in the family for years!"

They stared at each other.

At last Jessie spoke.

"So we're probably *related*?"

"Certainly looks like it," said Finn, his jaw hanging open. "S'pose you must be my great-great-great-great aunt or something."

"Weird!" said Jessie.

"Spooky," agreed Finn. "Reckon I'd rather just think of you as a kind of long-lost sister."

A smile flickered across his face.

"Bit of an age gap, though. Not sure I can cope with a sister who's a hundred and fifty years older than me..."

"Not sure *I* can cope with a brother who's a hundred and fifty years *younger*," retorted Jessie.

She snorted with laughter.

A moment later Finn joined in, the muscles of his face aching strangely with the long-forgotten act.

"Can't remember when I last laughed like that!" gasped Jessie. "Seems like for ever."

"Must be a hundred and fifty odd years," said Finn. "And it feels like about that long for me, too. Hasn't exactly been a laugh a minute at my place recently."

He glanced towards the cavern entrance.

"Did a good job at drowning out the flood, too. You've got one loud voice on you, you know."

"So have you," said Jessie.

She exploded in a fresh peal of giggles.

"Loud enough to wake the Dead, Finn Oliver!"

✳   ✳   ✳

It seemed as if he'd been crawling for hours.

Always there was another bend, another twist, another turn.

Every so often the tunnel walls would glow dimly with a patch of cooling algae and a new stretch of passageway would loom up in front of him.

Otherwise Morgan groped his way forward in pitch darkness.

The air temperature had plummeted and he knew he was losing form and colour with every passing second.

Already, the tips of his fingers were no more than smudges on the ends of whitened sticks and his magnificent red hair had bleached and thinned.

His strength was waning too.

He needed heat and he needed it fast.

If he failed to find help soon he would dwindle to nothing.

Morgan stopped in his tracks and listened.

An odd, irregular knocking sound was reverberating in the distance.

As he hauled himself around the next corner, the noise became louder and clearer – a hollow clanking resonating along the passageway and filling his ears with hope.

Not far off, a dim light signalled the end of the tunnel.

The passage had opened up enough now for Morgan to struggle the final distance on his feet.

Another twenty yards and it was upon him –

a long cavern, its yellow stalactites reaching down like ancient forefingers from the pitted rooftop.

At first glance it was very nearly familiar.

At least it was if he forced his eyes away from the cavern floor.

Because that was where everything went wrong.

Horribly, horribly wrong.

The whole place was awash with a paraphernalia of half-known objects.

A china doll lay on top of a toy garage; a rusty suit of armour vied for space with a single broken roller skate; a small pink fridge jostled against a golden shield...

And in the centre of it all bobbed a bright red Ford Fiesta.

Morgan's brain screamed into action.

Of course.

It was the car belonging to that sad excuse of a mortal.

He had found his way through some long-concealed tunnel into the Museum of Artefacts.

Just to his right a mammoth tusk had become wedged in the spokes of a rusty old bicycle.

To his left a drinking horn nestled inside an ornate Victorian pram.

And near the back of the cavern he could just make out a floating mass of Christmas decorations, all red baubles and glittery stars and plastic santas.

Up the walls of the Museum the water inched like stealthy fingers.

It was no longer a place for human presence.

The visitors of the Underworld had long since fled.

All except one man.

Morgan spotted him out of the corner of one eye.

The palest of pale figures floating towards him on a wooden crate, clutching an armful of glinting treasure to his chest.

He was whimpering like a small child.

For a second Morgan frowned at the fading scarlet robes, the grizzled hair, the withered stature.

And then he let out a strangled cry.

To one side of the figure hung a small, blood-stained axe.

✳ ✳ ✳

Edric swept back into the Chamber in a whirlwind of flying rosary beads.

"It's getting really nasty out there!" he cried, hurrying over to Finn and Jessie. "But I've had my recharge at the Igneous Fountain and it's done me the world of good. Just need to sort out those cuts of yours and then we can get moving, Master Oliver! There's no sign of Bloodaxe, by the way. No one seems to have a clue where he's got to."

He began ferreting around on a shelf crammed with jars and bottles of every shape and size.

"And Miss Sherratt," he added over his shoulder, "this time I really am dropping you off at the Red Temple on our way through. No arguments. Lady Fortescue's waiting for you. She's doing a fantastic job up there. Got everyone singing along to her old favourites. They were blasting through the chorus of *Oh my darling, Clementine* when I left. Raising their spirits no end."

Jessie cowered in the corner.

"But—" she began.

"No BUTS!" snapped Edric, turning to glare at her. "You heard me, Miss Sherratt! No arguments! No chickening out … no…"

He tailed off, his mouth hanging open.

"But Miss Sherratt! Why aren't you…? Why haven't you…? Surely by now you…?"

Finn and Jessie looked at each other uneasily as Edric banged the palm of his hand against his forehead.

"Fool!" he muttered. "*Fool!* How could I have been so stupid? Why didn't I guess? What with Master Oliver hanging on to his breathing down here, of course there had to be a side effect for you, too! *For every action there is an equal and opposite reaction.*"

Finn cleared his throat.

"Would you mind filling us in here?" he said.

Edric pointed at Jessie.

"Just look at her!" he shouted. "Is she fading away? Is she losing her colour? Is she blurring round the edges? I don't think so! Ooooooh no! She's resplendent! She's dazzling! She's ablaze with colour!"

Jessie stared down at herself, blinking at her own newly-discovered brightness.

"You still don't get it, do you?" squealed Edric, now practically bouncing up and down with excitement. "But it's so simple! So deliciously simple!"

He began to hover around the Chamber in ever-decreasing circles.

"I told you earlier that when I did the Reverse Heat Transfer I stopped just short of the complete operation. Quite deliberately, you understand. Left you with a scrap of coldness in your blood, Master Oliver. A morsel of the Dead. Just so as you could keep on breathing down here. After all, we didn't want a corpse on our hands, did we?"

He chuckled to himself and turned to Jessie.

"And though I didn't know it at the time, Miss Sherratt, you were given a bonus in the process, too. You were left with some of Master Oliver's precious mortal heat. And it's there in your system for keeps!

Nothing can take it away from you. Not even these confounded floods."

Jessie's eyes widened.

"So whatever it is that's worrying you about that water out there, you can put it right out of your mind! As long as you don't actually touch the stuff, you're immune! Saved! It simply cannot cool your spirit. You'll be floating about this joint long after the rest of us have disappeared into thin air. Who would've thought it, eh?"

Edric winked at her and glided back to the shelf of jars and bottles.

"However," he continued, selecting a small green phial and screwing up his eyes to check the label, "I'm afraid the rest of us have no such luck. I need to get Master Oliver out of here fast if I'm going to make it all the way to and from the upper passageways in time. Shouldn't think that recharge at the Fountain has bought me much more than another twenty minutes' extra floating."

He unstopped the little bottle and inverted its contents on to his fingertip.

"Premium cowslip juice," he announced. "Always take the opportunity to stock up on the flowers when I make a summer Ascent. Come on then, Master Oliver! Let's get it over with before we brave that cesspit of a flood."

Finn tore his eyes away from Jessie and winced as Edric smeared the sweet-smelling cowslip juice on to a deep cut just above his eye.

Behind them, the mixture inside the cauldron was working itself up into a bright blue frenzy.

"Hang on a second!" said Edric, setting down the bottle of cowslip remedy and fumbling for a long silver ladle that hung from a hook on the wall. "The Magmaplastic Solution's having one of its crazy fits. Need to give it a quick stir or it'll explode all over the place."

He plunged the ladle into the frothing liquid.

"Pity," he murmured. "Another few days and I might've worked it out. Had real potential, that did."

Finn looked on as Edric battled with the swirling mass.

"What's it for?" he asked. "Why is it so special?"

"It's special," said Edric, "because it might just have saved us from all this."

He gestured towards the floodwaters, which now lapped menacingly at the Chamber entrance.

"You mean it would have given us protection?" said Jessie. "Like the Firepearl?"

Edric shook his head.

"No, no," he said. "Not like the Firepearl at all. That would have given us everlasting protection. The Firepearl would quite literally have saved us

158

for ever. My Magmaplastic Solution could only have bought us a bit of time. Helped hold up the membrane till the worst of the storms had passed."

He gazed into the cauldron.

"It was designed to strengthen the Exit membrane, you see," he explained. "Would've worked like a kind of super-strength glue, if only I'd got the formula right. But I'm afraid there was something missing every time I had a shot at it."

"It's a fantastic colour, though," said Finn. "What's in it to make it so blue?"

"Essence of forget-me-not. The flower that speaks of eternal remembrance. Plucked from the meadows of the Other Side by my own fair hands."

The little monk began to sniff loudly.

"And what else is in there?" asked Jessie hastily.

"Secret recipe," muttered Edric. "A bit of this and a bit of that…"

"Oh come *on*!" said Finn. "Surely you can tell us *now*!"

Edric sighed.

"It's basically just a strong sugar solution," he said. "Plus the essence of forget-me-not and a single crushed cocoa bean. Sugar and love and a bit of chocolate thrown in for good measure. All the things necessary for human existence. I must've been so very close to cracking it, but it kept going all blue and bubbly on me – and I was after something much darker and stickier. Consistency of treacle, I suppose. It's been driving me mad."

"And now it's too late?" asked Finn.

"Wouldn't put it quite like that," said Edric. "Never too late for anything in my book. Might have a brainwave while I'm hovering here talking to you, mightn't I?"

He paused and fiddled with his string of rosary beads.

"But let's just say it's looking a little unlikely. Seems nature has caught up with us all at long last."

Edric glanced nervously at the doorway to the Chamber as a tongue of water spilled over the top step and trickled into the cavern.

"We're running out of time," he muttered. "We need to get out of here. Let me clean up that gash on your arm before we go, Master Oliver. Looks a bit nasty. Best deal with it in case you have to swim the final stretch through to the upper passageways."

A septic dribble of blood and pus had begun to ooze from the deepest of Finn's wounds all the way down to his left wrist.

"Give me your arm," instructed Edric. "Come on! Hold it over the cauldron! I need to keep stirring this wild gloop while I do it. And don't look like that – it won't bite!"

Finn inched his arm over the rim of the cauldron and Edric doused the weeping cut in a generous dollop of cowslip juice.

A final trickle of blood dropped into the mixture below and then the gash closed back up, leaving nothing but clear skin.

"Amazing!" said Finn. "I couldn't have some to take with me to the Other Side, could I? Might teach those doctors a thing or two…"

But Edric didn't answer. He wasn't even listening.

His eyes were riveted to the cauldron of Magmaplastic Solution.

Finn and Jessie followed his gaze.

Where moments before the cauldron had been full to bursting with sparkling blue liquid, now only a smattering of treacly black sludge clung to its base like burned caramel.

Edric shook his head slowly from side to side.

"The missing ingredient! I don't believe it! So there really *is* something mystical about that membrane … we've cracked it at last! At long, long last!"

He closed his eyes.

"Human blood!" he whispered. "Fresh human blood!"

8.
Bloodaxe

"Father!" screamed Morgan. "Father! Wait! It's me, Morgan!"

His voice blasted over the sea of objects and ricocheted off the opposite wall of the Museum.

But the figure sailed on by, lost to everything but the rhythm of its private lament.

"My gold! My silver! My sword! My bright, bright jewels!"

Bloodaxe cradled his treasure in his arms and rocked it like a baby.

"You will not be lost to me! My dears, my own, my rightful treasure!"

Morgan lowered himself to the ground and hung out over the mouth of the tunnel as far as he dared.

He waited for a lull in his father's melancholy

chanting and then cried out once more.

"Father! Listen to me! I need you to help me!"

Very slowly Bloodaxe turned, his face sunken and sallow.

Relief flooded Morgan.

His father had seen him.

He would take him aboard the little raft and together they would make it.

Drag themselves against the quickening current to the higher chambers of Exit 43.

Find their way to the Red Temple.

To the heat of the Igneous Fountain.

To the very last place the flood would seek them out.

Bloodaxes together.

Father and son.

The very best of Viking men.

Everything was going to be all right now.

Everything was going to turn out just fine.

✳   ✳   ✳

"Does this mean it might not be too late after all?" said Finn. "Does this mean there's still a chance?"

Edric shook himself out of his reverie and turned to Finn.

"Still a chance of what?" he asked sharply.

"Of me fulfilling the Prophecy of the Firepearl,

of course. Now you've worked out the formula and can stop the flood down here."

The little monk's face grew solemn.

"That depends," he said.

"Depends on what?"

"On everything," said Edric. "On whether there's a break in the storm for a start. On whether I can make it up as far as the membrane to coat it with Magmaplastic Solution. And of course it depends very much on what it's like down in the Gateway."

He paused.

"But most of all, Master Oliver, it depends on you. No one else can make a decision like this. It's a terrible risk to take."

"So don't even *think* about it, Finn," cut in Jessie. "It's *way* too dangerous. You need to get back to your mum, remember."

Finn stared down at his trainers.

"I need you to tell me something," he said, looking up at last and meeting Edric's gaze. "There's something I still don't understand. Something Mr Bloodaxe didn't really explain properly to me."

"Fire away," said Edric. "I'll tell you whatever you want to know."

"It's about those special stars. It's about the Inflammati."

"What about them?"

Finn kicked at a loose piece of rock on the floor of the cavern.

"Mr Bloodaxe said that if the Fires weren't saved, then the Inflammati would be lost, too. That's true, is it?"

Edric clenched his teeth.

"Blackmail!" he seethed. "Blackmail, pure and simple!"

"But is it true?"

"True enough," said Edric. "The legend tells that the release of the Firepearl will give everlasting protection to the Fires. And the Fires and the Inflammati have been linked together since time began. So I'm afraid it follows that if the Fires are quenched, there will be no Inflammati. They will be snuffed out one by one. Bloodaxe *is* right. Of course he's right. But I don't like his reasoning. I don't like it one little bit."

"But surely it's exactly what you want, too," said Finn, frowning. "For me to go through the dome of flames with a child of the Underworld and release the Firepearl. Save the Fires ... save the Inflammati ... save the Underworld ... save everything all in one go. Seems simple enough to me."

Edric sighed.

"The one thing I'm afraid it is not," he said, "is simple. Down there you'll be dicing with death –

there's no doubt about it. And so it's absolutely vital that you consider this extremely carefully. Work out what's right for you. You must follow your heart, dear boy. You must always follow your heart."

Finn flinched.

"What's the matter? What did I say?"

"Nothing," muttered Finn. "Just that thing about following your heart. I've heard it a few times before, that's all."

"Well, whoever you've heard it from is quite right," said Edric. "Because you can't live your life any other way. And if that involves making up your mind that the challenge of the Firepearl is the right thing for you, then all well and good…"

He folded his arms across his habit.

"However, what I cannot abide is some dirty tricks campaign on the part of Mr Harald Bloodaxe. I don't care how much we might need saving down here – the life of a mortal is infinitely more precious than the desires of a collection of desperate old ghosts. Bloodaxe had no right to try and force you into taking up the challenge. No right whatsoever."

"No one's going to force me into doing anything," said Finn, ignoring Jessie's steely glare. "I've made my decision. I made it ages ago. Just looked like it was going to get washed away with the flood, that's all."

He fixed his eyes on Edric.

"I'm doing it," he said. "I'm taking up the challenge. And nothing anyone says will make me change my mind."

Edric stared back at him.

"In which case," he said slowly, "we need to get this show rolling. Starting with me getting over to the Exit Tunnel and painting the membrane with Magmaplastic Solution just as soon as there's a lull in the storm."

Jessie darted forward.

"But you can't, Edric. You're fading away already. Even if you climb the ladders to the halfway point, you'll have to float the rest of the way up to the membrane. It must be hundreds and hundreds of feet to the top."

"Nine hundred and eighty-five," replied Edric. "To be precise."

Jessie gulped.

"Well, you'll never make it," she said. "It'll zap every last shred of energy from you, and you know it."

"Got anyone else in mind for the job?" said Edric, raising his eyebrows sarcastically.

"Yes," said Jessie. "Me. I'll seal the membrane. Seems like I'm the only person left down here who'll stand a chance anyway. Resplendent, that's how you described me earlier. Resplendent and dazzling."

Edric and Finn gaped at her.

"*You?*" cried Edric. "Don't be ridiculous, Miss Sherratt. It's been bad enough persuading you to come back with me over the floods as far as the Red Temple. Have you any *idea* what things will be like in the Exit Tunnel? It'll be worse than one of those horrible new-fangled water parcs they've built on the Other Side. You will have learned about those for your Exit Exam, yes? All flumes and waterfalls and nasty fake whirlpools. Except this time it'll be the real thing. It'll be turmoil … mayhem … chaos…"

Jessie pursed her lips.

"All right," she admitted. "I'll be scared. Of course I'll be scared. But I'll beat it. I'm stronger than the water, aren't I? That's what you said."

"Reckon I might've been running away with myself a bit there," said Edric. "Certainly the extra heat in your system will keep you hovering above the water. You're not going to fade away like the rest of us. But you absolutely mustn't make contact with the stuff. And that'll be almost impossible to avoid in the Exit Tunnel. There'll be water just pouring down between the ladders … waves bashing against the cave walls … drifting spray … the lot…"

"And if it does touch me?"

Edric shrugged.

"Who can say?" he said. "I suppose you might get away with the odd splash or two. But any more than that and you'll be done for."

"I'll take the chance," said Jessie. "I *have* to take the chance. I've got just as much to lose as the rest of you if we don't defeat this flood. It's hardly going to be a picnic wafting around down here by myself if everyone else disappears, is it? Won't be getting to see my family again *at all* the rate things are going."

She turned to Finn.

"And once I've dealt with the membrane I'll come with you to the Gateway and accompany you through the dome of flames. If that's OK with you, that is."

Finn blushed.

"Actually, I was kind of hoping you might volunteer," he said. "Didn't want to ask – what with you being so frightened of the water and everything."

"I've just told you," said Jessie. "I'm going to be fine. So that's everything settled. We'll leave Edric at the Red Temple and head straight for the Exit Tunnel. You can wait for me at the bottom of the ladders, Finn."

Edric glanced at Finn.

"What d'you reckon?" he asked.

"You heard what she said," replied Finn. "Sounds like she's made up her mind already."

Edric's eyes flitted between Jessie and Finn.

"You're quite, quite sure? Both of you? You know what you're taking on here?"

"Oh yes," said Finn, "we know what we're taking on."

"And you'll look after yourselves?"

"We'll look after ourselves," said Jessie. "And we'll look after each other, too. Because we're in this together."

* * *

Bloodaxe gaped at Morgan.

"Who are you, boy?" he croaked, hugging his glittering treasure close. "What brings you to these Viking lands? What brings you to my watery plains?"

Morgan blinked.

This wasn't the father he knew.

This wasn't the fierce and fiery man he had feared from his cradle.

This was a child … a lunatic … a madman…

A madman who apparently didn't even recognize his own son.

He forced himself to go on.

"It's me, Father. Morgan. Your only son."

"My son?"

Bloodaxe frowned.

"I believe I did once have a son," he mused. "Useless good-for-nothing wretch he was, too. Hated him from the instant I set eyes on him. Stole my Viking woman from me. Ripped her apart at the very moment of his loathsome birth."

He began to howl, bent double over his stash of treasure.

Morgan sprang to his feet.

Somehow he must keep his cool.

The crate-raft was only feet away from the entrance now.

In a few seconds it would be clear of the Museum and taking its chances on the flooded passageways outside.

"You've got to help me, Father! You've got to take me with you! Back to the Red Temple where it's safe and dry."

Bloodaxe stared at him.

"Red Temple?" he sniffed, confusion etched in every line of his harrowed face. "Never heard of it, boy. These are Viking lands I sail on. Flooded Viking lands. We Vikings rule the wide, wide world."

Morgan scanned the clutter of floating artefacts.

There had to be another way out of here.

If he could just make it to the nearest object.

Climb aboard and make a bid for safety.

Strike out on his own.

But already he could see that it was useless.

The current in the passageway outside was beginning to pull the exhibits towards it, stealing everything into its thieving grasp.

He would perish for certain if he jumped.

There had only ever been one way out.

And that was in the hands of this snivelling stranger.

Morgan stretched out his arms and called upon his father's mercy one final time.

✳   ✳   ✳

As they rounded the final corner to the Red Temple, Lady Fortescue's impromptu chorus was in full swing.

"*Oh my darling, oh my darling, oh my darling Clementine!*

Thou art lost and gone for ever, dreadful sorry, Clementine!"

"Very cheerful!" remarked Finn, shouting to make himself heard above the double din of the flood and the singing. "I *don't* think!"

Above him, carrying a jarful of Magmaplastic Solution in one hand and a paintbrush in the other, Jessie laughed.

"You'd think she'd have chosen something a bit more upbeat, wouldn't you?" she said.

At the head of their little party, Edric hovered to a wobbly halt at the top of the stairway leading into the Red Temple and peered in.

"But it's doing them the world of good!" he cried, as a blast of welcome heat from inside the Temple boosted him an inch or two higher into the air. "Just look at William Shakespeare over there! He's singing his head off!"

Finn goggled at Edric.

He waded out of the icy water and up the steps.

"Did you say William Shakespeare? Did you really say…?"

"Over by the Fountain!" shouted Jessie. "The one with the red felt cap and yellow stockings."

"He's from Exit 43?"

Jessie shook her head.

"Exit 25, I think. Rumour has it he's been visiting a relative over this way. Must've got caught up in it all."

"Hate to interrupt, Miss Sherratt," said Edric, "but I'm afraid this is where I have to bid you farewell."

Finn glanced at him.

"Better make it quick, then," he said. "There's not a lot left of you. I didn't want to worry you, but that bead thing of yours started to disappear just before we left the Chamber."

Edric's hand shot up to his rosary.

"You're quite right," he said. "I can hardly feel a thing. One or two little bobbly bits, but that's about it. Definitely time I made a move."

He swished over to Jessie with a final surge of energy and planted a noisy kiss on the top of her head.

Finn took a step backwards.

"I'll pass on all that if it's OK by you," he muttered. "Not really my kind of thing."

"Then I suppose this is it," said Edric, his chin beginning to quiver. "This really is goodbye. Good luck, both of you. And thank you, from the bottom of my heart. You've no idea how much this means to me. How much it means to *all* of us."

Two fat ghostly tears slid down his cheeks.

"Never in all my living or dying days have I met such—"

"*Give over!*" yelled Finn. "Stop blubbering and get inside that Temple! And by the way, you're losing your habit. Can't be doing with a half-naked monk romping around the Underworld."

At his words, Edric launched himself over the threshold of the Red Temple, clutching his habit as he went and muttering to himself about his worldly vows.

Jessie frowned at Finn.

"That was really mean," she said. "His habit was fine, and you know it. Why did you have to say that?"

"I just don't like goodbyes, OK? Can't stand them, in fact."

"He was only—"

"Leave it, Jessie … just leave it."

They lapsed into an awkward silence and watched as Edric half floated, half stumbled into the throng of singing spirits and disappeared into their midst.

A moment later he reappeared, carried upon a sea of shoulders towards the Igneous Fountain and waving his arms in time to the final bars of *Oh my darling, Clementine*.

"You're right," murmured Finn. "I shouldn't have wound him up like that. It's my problem. Not his."

"I wouldn't worry," said Jessie. "He'll have forgotten all about it by now."

She grinned at Finn and waved the jar of Magmaplastic Solution in front of his nose.

"Right! Let's get a move on! Exit Tunnel, here we come!"

* * *

"But there's only room for one!" cried Bloodaxe. "Can't you see, boy? Only room for me and my priceless Viking treasure on this valiant little ship of mine!"

"But I'll perish, Father! Perish in the floods! Perish in the cold passageways of the Underworld!"

"Perish?" echoed Bloodaxe.

He gazed down at his treasure.

"What is a human child to the loss of Viking gold?

We are mere specks, boy. We count for nothing."

Morgan clenched what was left of his vanishing fingers.

"Nothing, Father? Am I really worth nothing?"

"Ignorant child," said Bloodaxe. "We must not waste our care on silly human things."

He rested his head against the heap of gold and silver in his lap.

"I tried that long ago. Gave my love. Gave my heart. But life was cruel and flung them back at me. Stole from me the object of my sweet affections. And so I learned to trust instead in pretty things."

"You could try to love me, Father…"

The Viking warrior's face creased into a bewildered frown.

He turned back towards the entrance to the Museum, where the stern of his raft was already nudging into the passageway outside.

"Come back!" roared Morgan. "Come back, Father!"

Bloodaxe lifted his hand and saluted the lonely figure behind him.

"Farewell, boy! Whoever you are! Farewell! I sail on Viking lands! On flooded Viking lands!"

He clasped his treasure to his robes.

And then he disappeared into the passageway, his bloodied axe trailing to one side.

✳   ✳   ✳

An unbroken column of ice-cold muddy water, more than six foot across, blasted down the Exit Tunnel and hammered into the centre of the cavern.

Waves raced each other to the walls, crashing against the golden ladders with a noise like gunfire and sending clouds of spray high into the air.

"Hold on to the wall, Finn!" screamed Jessie, hovering above the spray. "There's another wave coming!"

Finn snatched at a finger of rock jutting out from the wall of the Exit Tunnel and held his breath as a towering wave of filthy floodwater gathered speed and headed straight for him.

He felt his heartbeat quicken. This was scary. Apart from some of the really difficult climbing he'd done with Dad, he didn't think he'd ever been so frightened.

The wave struck, knocking him off his feet and dragging him under the neck-high water.

His arms and legs smashed against the cavern walls.

For a moment he lost all sense of direction.

Icy water was gushing into his open eyes and nostrils…

He was choking … drowning…

And then he sensed a human face rippling just

above him and groped towards it, his hands clawing the surface.

"You've got to go back!" Jessie was screaming, her luminous features twisted with fear. "The water level's risen like crazy. You're going to drown, I swear it. Go back to the Red Temple. Wait for me there!"

"Get up past the spray!" yelled Finn. "Float above it! Don't let it touch you!"

He pounded the water with his bruised limbs in an effort to keep his head clear of the heaving waves.

"But you've got to get out of here!" insisted Jessie.

Finn spat out a mouthful of dirty brown water.

"No chance," he gasped, his lips puckering at the taste. "We're in this together, remember. That's what we said. And I'm not about to do a runner at the first sign of trouble."

"*You call this the first sign of trouble?*"

"I'm going to swim underwater to the nearest ladder," said Finn, ignoring her. "It's the only chance I've got against these waves. You go on up to the membrane. Wait till there's a break in the storm. I'll be here when you get back."

"And what if there's not a break in the storm?"

"Shut up, Jessie! You can't think like that! Just get up there!"

Already Finn was curling his body into a neat surface dive.

A second later he had disappeared, a shadowy figure gliding through the murky waters.

When he could hold his breath no longer he shot up for air.

Ahead of him a vast wave was sucking in on itself, preparing for the kill.

And between him and the arching wave was the first golden ladder, stretching ever upwards out of the water ... out of the fury ... out of the danger.

He had a couple of seconds at most.

Finn ducked back down and thrust himself at the ladder.

Any moment now ... surely, any moment now...

A flash of gold and his knuckles were buckling against hard metal.

He hauled himself clear of the water just as the wave hit, crushing the breath from his lungs and hurling him backwards.

His arms jarred in their sockets ... every sinew trembled...

But somehow he held his grip.

And then he was scrambling up the ladder, shivering with cold and gasping for air.

"You made it, then?"

Finn's head jerked upwards.

Just above him, Jessie was grasping hold of the ladder with one hand and cramming the paintbrush and jar of Magmaplastic Solution into the pocket of her crinoline with the other.

"What are you *doing* up there?" panted Finn, still struggling for breath.

"What does it look like I'm doing?" Jessie shouted back, already beginning to climb. "Getting myself up this ladder, of course. Just wanted to check you were OK before I got started."

"But you don't *have* to climb! That's the whole point."

Jessie continued to scale the rungs like a circus monkey.

"I'm going up every inch of this ladder. It's what we have to do when we make an Exit Ascent, in any case."

"But you're not *making* an Exit Ascent – and you're not making any sense either, come to that."

Jessie stopped climbing for a moment and scowled down at Finn over her shoulder.

"Use your brain, idiot!" she yelled against the raging torrent of floodwater. "Isn't it obvious why I want to go up the usual way? I'm terrified, OK? Terrified of falling … terrified of all this water … terrified of letting everybody down."

Finn gaped at her.

"But you seem so together – so calm."

"I'm putting on a brave face, aren't I? It's the only

way I can do it. The heat won't do it on its own. If I want to float once I reach the top of the ladders, then I have to believe in myself. And I'm trying to think positive thoughts, really I am, but it's not easy."

"Then why don't I come with you?" shouted Finn. "I could keep you company. I can climb this ladder no problem."

"There's no point! You can't go any further than the top rung, can you? And in any case, you need to conserve your energy for the journey to the Gateway."

Jessie turned back to the ladder.

"If you want to help, then see what you can do to distract me."

"Distract you?"

"Talk to me, Finn. Talk to me for as long as we can still hear each other."

"What about?"

"*Anything you like!* Just so long as it takes my mind off what I've got to do."

Finn cast about wildly for inspiration.

"Tell me about some of the other Exits, then!" he shouted, as another gigantic wave smashed into the ladder below them. "Tell me what they look like."

Jessie's voice came back small and muffled.

"Apparently the one just under New York's incredible. They updated it last year – gave it a complete overhaul. It sucks people up in a vortex of swirling pink steam and spins them off to the sound of famous American film stars whispering in their ears."

Beneath her, Finn couldn't help but roll his eyes.

"Where does it bring them out?" he yelled.

"Near the Statue of Liberty. Pretty cool, don't you think?"

"Wicked! How are you doing up there?"

"I'm fine! Just keep on talking…"

"I can hardly hear you…"

"And there's a new one … only just been discovered … below the Saudi Arabian desert … still testing out the Ascents. It's supposed to make you feel as if you're in the middle of a giant exploding sandcastle. Mr Glenridding told me it was…"

But whatever Mr Glenridding had told her was lost on Finn.

She was nothing but a tiny bright speck in the distance.

And for the first time since they had met, Finn and Jessie found themselves apart.

✳   ✳   ✳

Morgan stared around the ransacked Museum of Artefacts.

Almost everything had now either followed his father into the passageway or else sunk without trace beneath the surface of the rising water.

Even the mortal's car had finally bumped and smashed its way out of the Museum.

Morgan could picture it now – a great hunk of red metal, wedged against the walls where the passage tapered and narrowed a little further down.

A solid reminder of everything that could have been.

A symbol of the day the Underworld had so very nearly been saved – but instead had been lost for ever.

And for Morgan too, it had all been a complete waste of time.

His journey from the Gateway had brought him nothing but the bitter taste of rejection.

He knew that feeling well.

It was an old companion.

But in the past the bitterness had always given way to hope, to the belief that one day he would show his father exactly what he was made of.

This time he knew he was beaten.

And all that remained was to force himself back along the secret tunnel to the rocky shelf above the Gateway.

Because he wasn't going to perish here.

Not in this watery cavern of washed-up junk and treasure, where the last few survivors of the current's steady pull lay strewn before him – a stupid plastic doll, lying face-down in the water, its head half-severed from its body … an electric light bulb, trailing in its wake…

Morgan Bloodaxe wouldn't spend his final seconds in the company of a pile of useless rubbish, watching the entrance in some sad hope that his father would return to save him.

He would crawl back to the one place that meant something to him.

And amidst the coursing floodwaters and enchanted dome of curling flames he would buy himself a little comfort.

There would be the sound of the Fires, hissing and spluttering beneath him.

There would be the nearness of the hidden, useless Firepearl.

And there would be the golden Inflammati, dipping and dimming and dying in the vast darkness of eternity.

Perhaps he would stare up at them one more time.

Hold the whole host of fading stars in his gaze and dare, just for a single second, to imagine the mother he had never known.

Or perhaps he would not.

Perhaps he would simply harden his heart one last notch.

And perish alone.

9·
The Journey
to the Gateway

This time there was no voice to shout out instructions when she got to the top of the ladder.

The moment her hand finally met with thin air, Jessie knew she was in this on her own.

Ahead of her, illuminated by the searing brightness of her own being, she could just make out the column of floodwater as it hurtled down the centre of the Exit Tunnel.

And yet she could hear nothing.

She was in no-man's-land, a limbo between the Other Side and the Underworld, a halfway house between life and death.

Jessie gripped the uppermost rung and allowed the rest of her body to drift away from the ladder.

So far, so good.

But it was the next bit she was dreading.

It was all very well wafting around the passageways of Exit 43.

Quite another to let go this far up with nothing but a jet of filthy water for company.

She was beginning to regret her original plan.

It would've been far better to float up from the base of the Exit Tunnel, just as Finn had said.

Nice, steady progress rather than this sudden, terrifying lurch into nothingness.

But that was the path she had chosen.

Just so long as you believe in yourself, you'll be fine. The heat will do the rest…

Slowly, Jessie uncurled her fingers from the rung – and executed a perfect hover in mid-air.

Lightheaded with relief, she rolled herself clear of the ladder and began to circle the pillar of cascading water.

Was it simply her imagination or was the force of the water beginning to slow just a fraction?

The stream was surely narrowing…

Jessie didn't stop to consider another moment.

If this was the lull in the storm they'd all been hoping for, then she had to get moving fast.

She covered the final distance in seconds, soaring towards the membrane like a blazing comet.

By the time she reached it, the water had receded

to a gentle flow and within a few minutes no more than a trickle was coming off the moor.

The trickle turned to a drip.

And through the gap in the Earth's crust there shone a pale shaft of sunlight.

With shaking hands, Jessie reached for the jar of Magmaplastic Solution and unscrewed the lid.

She would not let herself look up.

She would not feast her eyes upon the Other Side.

She would concentrate on this single task – get on with the job in hand.

Plunging the paintbrush into the jar, Jessie smeared the tarry glue on to the edge of the membrane.

Almost at once it began to weave back in on itself, its snapped gossamer threads seeking each other out and twisting together to form a fine mesh.

She dipped the brush back into the jar and slathered on another generous dollop of Solution.

Soon she was working to a steady rhythm – dipping and coating, dipping and coating – until just a chink of light remained.

Jessie angled the paintbrush into the final, awkward corner of torn membrane.

And it was then that she made her fatal mistake.

Out of the corner of one eye she glimpsed a tantalizing flash of moor.

It was bleak and cold and wet.

But she could taste the peaty earth upon her lips … smell the musky gorse … hear the rustle of the windswept heather…

And a stab of pure longing shot through her heart.

She jammed the paintbrush back into the near-empty jar and raised her face to the weak sun.

The next minute her free hand had followed her gaze, shooting upwards through the tiny gap in the membrane.

And then she was snatching at the grass and the gorse and the heather … scrabbling at the storm-torn moor for a scrap of earth … something … anything … to take back with her into the Underworld. A reminder of everything she had lost … everything she had missed out on…

And in her frenzy the forgotten jar of precious Magmaplastic Solution slithered from her grasp and skittered away down the Tunnel – taking with it the very last scraping of healing glue.

✳   ✳   ✳

In the time it had taken Morgan to crawl to and from the Museum of Artefacts, everything had changed in the Gateway.

Clouds of angry black smoke rose up from the depths of the Earth as the Fires hissed their hatred of the quenching floods.

The air was pinched and raw.

And above him, though he had not yet dared to look, Morgan sensed a terrible darkening of the heavens.

Only the dome of silver flames remained unaltered, ever faithful to its precious inmate.

He glanced down at himself. Already he was little more than the greyest of shadows.

And so the time had come.

Morgan tilted his face to the roof of the Gateway and prepared to open his heart the tiniest crack.

But scarcely had he begun to focus his fading eyes through the fault in the rock than a scream splintered the blackening air.

A brutal snarl of a cry.

A cry of hideous awakening.

Morgan wrenched his gaze from the canopy of stars and opened his mouth in a silent howl of his own.

A wooden crate was spinning down the Gateway steps towards the dome of enchanted flames, all trace of madness wiped from its rider's face.

The silvery fire beckoned with stinging arms.

And by its pale light Morgan saw just one thing reflected in the eyes of its hastening prey.

Terror.

✳   ✳   ✳

Jessie nosedived down the Exit Tunnel in a single swoop.

"Did you see where it landed?" she screamed at Finn, shooting past him and scanning the surface of the dark water.

Finn was swinging backward and forward on the ladder and grinning from ear to ear.

"You did it!" he whooped. "It's all stopped! You are *so* cool, Jessie Sherratt!"

"*It's only stopped because the storm's stopped!*" she cried. "*Did you see where it landed?*"

Finn stopped swinging and stared at her.

"Did I see where what landed?"

"The jar of Magmaplastic Solution."

Finn's eyes widened.

"The jar?"

"I dropped it. I let go of it before I'd finished sealing the membrane…"

"Before you'd finished sealing the membrane?"

"*Will you stop repeating everything I say?* I made a stupid mistake, all right? I was trying to reach over on to the Other Side. I was trying to get a bit of earth…"

"A bit of earth?"

Jessie glared at him.

"Sorry … sorry … but I don't understand. What would you want with a bit of earth?"

190

"I wanted to bring something back, didn't I?" muttered Jessie. "Something to remind me. Just a little piece of life. Stupid of me, I know — and so selfish."

Finn chewed on his thumbnail and sighed.

"Well, I definitely didn't see anything land. It's almost completely dark down here without you, remember. And it will have sunk by now. So I reckon we can forget about trying to find that jar."

He looked at her doubtfully.

"I suppose we could go back and see if there's any Solution left in Edric's Chamber. Might just be a bit stuck to the bottom of the cauldron."

Jessie shook her head.

"No chance," she said. "You saw how little there was once it reacted with your blood. Edric scraped out every last speck. He'd have to boil up another batch. And we can't afford to wait around while he does that. All this water will be draining down towards the Fires…"

She broke off.

"Should've thought about this earlier, shouldn't I?" she whispered. "If only I'd kept my head up there."

Finn stretched over to take her hand, flinching as his fingers met with nothing but particles of light.

"What you did was really brave, Jessie. Like you said, the last bit was just a stupid mistake."

"A mistake that might cost us everything. All it'll

take is another burst of heavy rainfall and the membrane will rip apart where it's still hanging open – and then we'll be back to square one."

They stared at each other in silence.

"We'll just have to make the best of it," said Finn at last. "It's all we can do."

They both started as a fresh drizzle of rainwater fell between the ladders.

"And right now," Finn went on, dropping back down into the flooded base of the Exit Tunnel and eyeing the wavering stream of brown water, "that means keeping focused and getting ourselves down to the Gateway as fast as possible. Come on – if we're lucky you might still have bought us enough time."

And with Jessie gliding above him as his guiding light, Finn began to swim out of the Exit Tunnel towards the passageways that lay beyond…

They were just passing the Red Temple when he yelled at Jessie to stop.

"Something's wrong!" he cried, hauling himself out of the water and up the steps. "It's gone all quiet in the Temple. The singing's stopped."

Together they peered in through the entrance.

The fading spirits of Exit 43 were holding each other close.

Families, friends, strangers – all were huddled together in little groups.

And the singing had given way to the sound of muted weeping.

In one corner Glenridding clasped Lady Fortescue in a tender embrace, her cheek against his shoulder, his hand stroking her hair.

Edric trailed from group to group, murmuring soft words of comfort.

And in the very centre of the cavern, where a stream of fiery molten rock should have been rocketing into the air, there was nothing but silence.

Jessie's eyes filled with an icy fear.

"It's the Igneous Fountain," she said. "It's gone out. And you know what that means, don't you?"

She bent her head and covered her face with her hands.

"It means the Fires must be very nearly out themselves," she whispered. "It means it's all going to be too late."

∗　∗　∗

The flames made short work of their quarry, grasping Bloodaxe for a split second of exquisite torment and then casting him from their barbed jaws into the eddying floodwaters.

His tortured remains quivered for a moment on the scummy surface, as if pleading for a glimmer of mercy.

But the water desired only to finish off the job.

It clamoured for its human fragment, roaring and ravenous.

And on his ledge, Morgan cradled his own shrivelling shadow to himself and watched his Viking father perish.

He saw the final scrap of faded scarlet robes dissolve.

The once proud forehead twitch and spasm.

The sneering upper lip fall in upon itself.

The warrior spirit droop and crumple.

Until only a wasted hand remained … and the tip of a blood-stained axe…

And then nothing.

Nothing.

✳   ✳   ✳

Finn dashed back down the steps.

"How much further?" he yelled at Jessie. "How much further to the Gateway?"

"Don't ask me!" she snapped. "I've never been down there, have I?"

He twisted round to face her.

"*Never been down there? Now* you tell me, Jessie Sherratt. And there I was thinking you were the expert…"

"I'm a Novice, Finn. I've only been here three weeks. I don't know anything much. Just that you get there through the passageway leading from the Museum of Artefacts."

Finn plunged back into the biting-cold floodwater.

"Come on!" he cried. "I need you ahead of me to light the way."

"But it's too risky! You'll get trapped down there! And it's too late anyway."

"We're not giving up!" gasped Finn, already cutting through the seething waters. "Not when we've got this far. Not when we've got so much to lose."

Jessie hovered as close to the surface of the water as she dared.

"And what exactly *have* you got to lose, Finn Oliver? I still don't get what's in this for you."

Finn pressed on past the turning for Edric's Chamber – then flipped over on to his back to draw breath.

"I can't explain why I've got to do it," he said. "I don't really know why myself, OK? I just know I should be saving those Fires of yours, that's all."

"Ah, but it's the Inflammati you're really interested in, isn't it?" said Jessie. "That's what's at the bottom of all this. It's because your dad's up there, right?"

"I guess," muttered Finn, his teeth chattering madly. "But I want to help you, too."

He struck out through the floodwaters once more.

"But it's not as if you'll even be able to *see* the Inflammati when you get back to the Other Side," persisted Jessie. "*If* you get back to the Other Side... Surely it can't be worth risking your life over?"

"I'm following my instincts," panted Finn. "And right now they're screaming at me to get to the Gateway and release that Firepearl."

As they approached the Museum of Artefacts Finn stopped again and trod water, his breath coming in noisy rasps.

"Are you OK?" asked Jessie, frowning.

"Just catching my breath ... water's so cold ... and there's an undercurrent ... keeps trying to suck me down ... but I'm fine..."

Jessie looked at him anxiously.

"You don't look fine to me," she said. "You look completely knackered."

Finn turned away and clutched at the side of the passageway for support.

"Hang on a minute!" shouted Jessie. "There's something up ahead of us. Look! Something's wedged in the passage."

"It's Mum's car!" cried Finn. "It's floated out of the Museum!"

"And there's a load of things stacked up behind it! All the exhibits must've been sucked out of the entrance!"

Finn picked his way through the floating mass of objects and hauled himself on to the roof of the car.

"Just need a breather," he gasped. "Just a few seconds' rest… "

Jessie circled above him.

"What's in there, then?" she asked, pointing to the car boot. "What do twenty-first century mortals keep in the back of their cars? Parasols? Picnic rugs?"

"*Parasols?*" choked Finn. "*Picnic rugs?* I don't think so! More likely to be a pair of old climbing boots and a spare tyre in this one…"

He broke off and stared at Jessie, open-mouthed.

"*The spare tyre!* Of course!"

Finn hung off the roof and began to fumble with the catch on the car boot.

"There's an inner tube in with the spare tyre! I'm sure of it. It got used for a temporary repair job. All I need now is a foot-pump to blow it up with."

The boot sprang open and Finn clambered in.

"Yes!" he yelled, punching the air. "Just as I'd hoped. One inner tube. One foot-pump. One amazing piece of luck."

He pulled out his trophies and climbed back on to the roof of the car.

"I've found myself a lifebelt, Jessie," he said. "Once I've pumped this up, it'll carry me down to the Gateway, no problem."

Soon he was brandishing the inflated inner tube above his head.

"Time to get moving again!" he cried, launching himself back into the water. "And you'd better put on some speed this time, Jessie Sherratt!"

He careered down the passageway, buoyed up by his home-made lifebelt and immune to the grasping undercurrent beneath him.

Jessie sailed along just in front, lighting the way.

They sped into the depths of the Underworld, hurtling along the passage until at last they caught the telltale stench of stinging smoke.

But as they approached the steps leading to the Gateway, a low growl at their backs had them wheeling round.

A gigantic bank of water was rolling towards them…

"It's given way again!" cried Jessie. "The membrane's torn apart!"

Finn stretched up a hand.

"Quick!" he yelled. "Take my hand and don't let go! We might still beat it…"

They spun down the narrow stairway, Finn rotating on the lifebelt and preparing to trust his life to a hand he could not feel.

The thick smoke rising from the Fires now shrouded the cavern in a suffocating black cloak.

Only the dazzling light from Jessie's spirit shone out amidst the fog of grime and soot.

They didn't see the pale human shape watching from the rocky shelf above.

They didn't see the deadly aim of its launch as it cast what was left of its fragile form through the inky air.

They didn't see the look of triumph light up its ashen face – not until it was right upon them, grabbing the spare flesh of Finn's outstretched hand in its own and pitching all three of them forward into the dome of cavorting flames.

10.

The Four Challenges

"You again?" yelled Finn, as they breached the wall of flames together. "Should've guessed I hadn't seen the last of you, Morgan Bloodaxe!"

His lifebelt vanished at the touch of the fire and he looked down to see himself standing on a bed of silvery flames. The commotion in the Gateway fell away to nothing as he was enfolded in a silent, warm embrace.

Don't let go of Jessie's hand, whatever you do … remember the words of the Prophecy … without immortal protection I'll be roasted alive…

Morgan leered at Finn.

Already the heat was starting to feed its way back into him, pumping him full of energy and colour.

"Good to see you too, Mortal Boy! Looks like

we've got through the barrier, doesn't it? Reckon I might risk letting go now we're past the tricky bit. Thanks for the lift!"

He released his fingers from Finn's hand and rose phoenix-like through the soaring tongues of magical fire.

"And New Girl, too!" he cried, grinning down at them both from above. "Take it you got back from your little outing over on the Other Side all right, then? Nice Mr Glenridding scraped you off the moor, did he?"

Jessie stared straight ahead of her, gimlet-eyed.

"Dare you to let go of him!" sniggered Morgan, twisting and turning with the pale flames. "Outgrown his usefulness now, hasn't he? His turn to rely on you, New Girl! Be a right laugh to watch him fry, don't you reckon?"

Finn and Jessie exchanged glances.

"Quite a surprise to see a Novice down here, I must say. Wouldn't have thought they'd want to let you loose on quite such a dangerous mission."

Morgan sighed.

"Still, I guess that's Management for you. Completely clueless half the time. Don't know whether they're coming or going."

"Doesn't say a lot for your father then, does it?" bit back Jessie, unable to contain herself any longer.

"Considering he's supposed to run the place."

The set of Morgan's spiteful face slipped.

"You want to watch that tongue of yours, New Girl," he snapped. "Better get one thing straight right now. No one criticizes my father. *No one.* Do I make myself clear?"

"Not especially," said Jessie. "I'm not too interested in your father, if you must know. Seems he's nothing but a nasty bully."

Morgan lunged at her.

"Touchy, aren't we?" said Jessie, as he shot straight through her and swooshed out the other side. "Well, you don't scare me, Morgan Bloodaxe."

"Where is your father, in any case?" asked Finn. "There wasn't any sign of him up at the Red Temple. I would've thought he'd have wanted to be right in the thick of it."

Morgan scowled at him.

"What would you know about anything, Mortal Boy? I expect my father had more important things to do than round up a load of dithering half wits. Left the dirty work to the likes of Glenridding and company."

He tossed back his hair.

"Now if you'll excuse me, I'd better not hang about. There's this Firepearl business to attend to … I'll race you to the finishing line…"

202

And he darted away through the leaping flames.

Jessie felt Finn's hand slipping from her grasp as he tried to dive after Morgan.

Just in time she caught him back.

"What d'you think you're playing at?" she yelled. "We're nearly there, Finn – I can see the end of the wall of fire… But until we get through this first challenge you mustn't take your hand away, OK? You have to keep contact with me!"

"Sorry," muttered Finn. "I just can't stand the thought of Morgan reaching the Firepearl first."

Jessie frowned.

"But the Firepearl has to be released by a mortal," she said firmly. "Even if Morgan does get to it first, he won't be able to *do* anything about it."

"I wouldn't be so sure," said Finn. "By hitching a lift through the flames, he's already turned the Prophecy on its head, hasn't he? There are three of us in this game now. And Morgan Bloodaxe is out to cause trouble, I'm sure of it."

He shook his head.

"I've got a bad feeling about this, Jessie," he said. "This isn't how it was supposed to turn out at all."

✳   ✳   ✳

Morgan raced ahead of them through the silvery flames, muttering to himself as he went.

Self-righteous idiots – the pair of them.

Who the hell did they think they were anyway, spouting off like that about his father?

Like they knew what had really happened to him.

Like they knew the true story.

But he mustn't let it get to him.

He had to keep his cool.

Especially now he'd been given a second chance.

Wasting away back there in the Gateway amidst the floods and the black smoke, he'd thought his dream was over for good.

He'd thought everything was over for good.

And then the impossible had happened.

Mortal Boy had come sailing down the steps straight into his arms.

And once again Morgan Bloodaxe had everything to play for.

True, he could no longer prove himself to his father.

Not that he wanted to think too hard about that.

In fact he didn't want to go there at all…

But there was everyone else to impress, wasn't there?

The poor folk of Exit 43 were going to need a new Head of Exit, after all.

And once he'd breezed through the rest of these stupid enchantments and swiped the Firepearl off Mortal Boy, he was going to be their number one man.

Only the girl stood in his way now.

It wouldn't do for her to witness him chucking Mortal Boy over the cliff to his death, would it?

Before he did anything else he had to get rid of her.

Oh yes – New Girl very definitely had to go.

✳   ✳   ✳

Finn and Jessie emerged from the flames on to a narrow footpath.

Morgan was nowhere to be seen.

To one side of the path a bright ribbon of fast-flowing water stretched away into the distance.

And immediately in front of them stood a wide stone bridge.

"The challenge of the water, I suppose," said Finn, frowning. "It feels as if we've left the Underworld behind us though, doesn't it? This is just like something you might find on the Other Side."

Beside him, Jessie had frozen.

"That's because it is," she whispered.

"Is what?"

"Is something you'd find on the Other Side. Or at least it's an enchanted replica of it. This is the river that starts near the Exit membrane, Finn. The one that runs right through the middle of the village. And this exact spot is where…"

Jessie broke off, her eyes wide and staring.

"It's – it's the place where I drowned."

Finn gaped at her.

"Are you sure?" he asked.

"Of course I'm *sure*," said Jessie, shuddering. "I know this place like the back of my hand. I spent nearly every day of my life messing about down here with my brother."

She glided up close to Finn as he stepped on to the bridge.

Behind them the footpath vanished into thin air.

"Seems the whole place is charmed," said Finn. "Bang goes any chance of cheating and walking alongside the river instead."

Jessie ran her fingers over the keystone of the bridge.

"Look!" she said, pointing to a series of initials etched into the stonework. "These are the names of all the children who've played here. And here are mine and Tom's – J.E.S. … T.F.S. … 13th March 1859. We scratched those in only a few days before the accident."

Finn squinted at the array of letters and numbers.

"Yours is the most recent date, too," he said. "This bridge has been frozen in time for us. It's exactly as it was the day you drowned."

Jessie glanced over her shoulder.

"What's up now?" snapped Finn. "Don't be so jumpy. You're freaking me out."

"I keep expecting Tom to appear. Can't help wondering if he's going to be part of the challenge."

Finn shook his head.

"I don't think so," he said more gently. "This isn't some sick replay of your death, Jessie. I reckon it's just a test of nerve. You're going to have to manage without your brother. You'll have to make do with me instead."

He jumped up and straddled the top of the bridge.

"*Watch out!*" screamed Jessie. "Are you *trying* to kill yourself or something?"

"I'm working out what we've got to do."

Jessie pulled a face at him.

"Isn't it obvious what we've got to do? We've got to get to the other end of the river, haven't we? It runs for about half a mile downstream to the watermill."

"*Half a mile?*"

Finn eyed the water as it surged beneath them.

Then he twisted round and began to lower himself over the side of the bridge.

"*Finn!*"

"I'm fine, Jessie. It'll be OK. I've had more than enough practice in the passageways."

"*The drop … it's such a long way down…*"

207

But Finn had already plunged into the river.

The iciness of the water shocked the breath out of him and for a while it was all he could do to stay afloat.

When at last he looked back to check on Jessie's progress, he saw that she was still on the bridge.

"Come *on!*" he cried. "We said we'd do this together, didn't we? Why are you so afraid?"

Jessie stared back mutely.

"You're already dead, Jessie. You can't break your neck twice. All you've got to do is float over the water. It's me who's got the raw deal here. Just get *moving!*"

With a supreme effort of will, Jessie shut her eyes and stretched out her arms.

The next moment, she was floating clear of the bridge.

For a few seconds it seemed that everything was going to be all right.

And then she started to drop.

"What's happening?" shouted Finn.

"I don't know!" cried Jessie. "I just know I can't do it... It feels like I'm right back there on the day I drowned ... the moment I lost my balance ... the lurching feeling in my stomach as I fell..."

"So New Girl *drowned*, did she?" jeered a familiar voice behind them. "Well, well – what a very *useful* piece of information."

Finn spun round in the water to see Morgan gliding towards them.

"Don't listen to him, Jessie!" he yelled. "Just remember what you told me earlier in the Exit Tunnel. If you want to float, then you have to believe in yourself, OK? You have to believe in your spirit powers."

Morgan made a retching noise above them.

"Oh, how *sweet!*" he drawled. "Did you hear that, New Girl? Did you hear what Mortal Boy said? You have to *believe* in yourself."

Jessie's gaze flicked towards Morgan.

"Not that it can be easy believing in yourself when you're so obviously such a total failure," he sighed. "Fancy getting yourself marooned on the Other Side on your very first Exit Ascent. Talk about messing up big time."

Shame filled Jessie's green eyes.

She sank still lower towards the surging waters.

"*Look at me, Jessie!*" screamed Finn, flailing wildly against the dragging current. "Who saved my life when I fell down the Exit Tunnel? Tell me that, Jessie Sherratt? Who saved my *life?*"

A tiny upwards movement in her shimmering figure spurred him on.

"Who agreed to paint the Exit membrane? Who lit the way through the passages? Who brought me through the enchanted flames?"

And with each question Jessie rose higher and higher above the treacherous water and into the safety of the air above.

"I did, Finn!" she cried, her spirit blazing with light and colour. "I did!"

✳   ✳   ✳

The quaint little watermill that marked the end of the river dissolved to nothing as Morgan approached and in its place a near-vertical sheet of rugged grey rock rose up from a stretch of solid ground.

The third challenge.

The challenge of the earth.

It would be child's play for a heat-filled spirit like him.

Morgan glanced over his shoulder to where Finn still thrashed through the water, New Girl floating above his head.

They were like best friends, those two.

Thick as thieves.

All that gross talk about believing in yourself — it was enough to make anyone puke.

Morgan sighed.

He knew he should have stuck around and had another go at New Girl.

Chucked a few more insults her way.

But he hadn't been able to stand it any longer.

He'd had to get away from all that *friendship*.

And there was still time, he reminded himself.

Still time to wipe New Girl off the map before it came to his big moment with Mortal Boy and the Firepearl...

And it was then that the thought sprang into Morgan's mind.

A new and glorious thought.

A thought so delicious that it filled him with a fresh surge of energizing heat.

What if he didn't need to hang around for the others after all?

What if by cadging a lift through the flames like that he had broken the magic of the Prophecy ... and he could release the Firepearl himself?

Morgan shot up the rock face in a trice.

A smooth plateau stretched out in front of him.

And in the distance he could make out the closing wall of enchanted flames.

He had to be very nearly there...

Above him, peeping through a minute gap in the dome of flames, he could just make out the constellation of the dying Inflammati.

Well, he wasn't going to waste time looking at them.

He didn't need any encouragement now.

Not from his father – and not from his mother, either.

Morgan Bloodaxe was invincible.

He needed no one.

And he would do this on his own.

He glided out across the plateau, lost in a vision of his glittering future.

And then he put on a surge of speed.

Something had caught his eye.

A tiny rose-coloured ball, a miniature evening sun of light, shimmering like a fragile bubble just an arm's length away from the end of the table-top of rock…

Finn stared at the rock face rearing up in front of him.

It was worse than anything he'd tackled before in his whole life. Worse than the advanced climbing wall back at the teaching centre in London. Worse even than the massive cliff he and Dad had climbed together a couple of summers' ago. At least that time he'd had all the right gear. And anyway, Dad had been with him then, hadn't he? He'd watched him every step of the way.

"I can't do it, Jessie," he said, hauling himself out of the icy water.

Jessie gaped at him.

"Can't do it? But what do you mean?"

Finn gestured towards the tower of rock.

"Just look at it," he said. "It's way too difficult. I wouldn't know where to begin."

Jessie followed his gaze.

"Come on, Finn," she said. "It's not that bad. Not compared with all the daredevil stuff you've done already. Not compared with walking through fire or surviving that terrible river."

"Oh, right!" snapped Finn. "So you'd be prepared to give it a go, would you? You'd chance it up there if you were just a mere mortal? You don't know anything about climbing, Jessie Sherratt. You haven't got the first clue. I learned how to do it properly with my dad, OK? And it's not easy, believe me. Even when you're strapped into a harness. Even when you've got someone at the top holding on to the rope."

He slumped down shivering at the foot of the rock.

"And this time there's no rope and no harness … and what's more, there's no Dad either."

"But how can you possibly give up now?" said Jessie. "After everything you said to me in the water … about how we have to believe in ourselves."

"Yeah," said Finn. "But I was talking about you, not me. I never said anything about believing in *myself*, did I? What Morgan said back there was right. You can't believe in yourself when you're a total failure."

LIBRARY
RESOURCE
CENTRE

"But you're not a failure!" cried Jessie. "Whatever makes you say that?"

Finn bent his head.

"It doesn't matter," he mumbled. "Nothing matters any more, Jessie. I feel empty. Hollow. I thought there must be some point to all this. Some reason for coming. But I was wrong. There's no point at all. There's no point to anything."

"But of course there's a point. You want to save the Inflammati, don't you? You want to save the memory of your dad…"

"*Shut up about my dad!*" shouted Finn. "Shut *up*, Jessie Sherratt! You haven't a clue what you're talking about."

He glared down at the ground.

"You don't know what it was like between him and me."

"You could try telling me."

Finn buried his face in his hands.

"Before the divorce we did everything together, OK?" he whispered fiercely. "Everything you could possibly imagine. I remember flying my first remote-controlled plane with him. Just the two of us on the top of a hill out in the countryside. We let the plane go and then raced down the hill to fetch it back. We did it all afternoon. It was magic."

Finn clenched his teeth against the memory.

"And after the split he was still there for me. As much as he could be, at any rate."

"Sounds like he was a fantastic dad."

"He was. He was brilliant – a bit mad, perhaps – but the best dad you could possibly imagine."

"So why isn't it worth trying to save his memory?"

"*Of course it's worth trying to save his memory.* It's not *him* that's the problem. I just told you, didn't I? It's me. I'm the problem. I'm nothing but a pathetic failure."

He looked miserably up at Jessie.

"You see, I haven't told you the worst of it."

"Haven't told me the *worst* of it?"

"I never said goodbye to him, Jessie. I never said goodbye to my dad."

"Well, of course you didn't say goodbye. You didn't know what was going to happen, did you?"

"I don't mean that…"

There was a moment's silence.

"I've never told anyone this before," muttered Finn. "Not even my mother – *especially* not my mother."

He began to fiddle with the drawstring of his father's anorak.

"Dad and I saw each other every Sunday," he said. "After the divorce, I mean. And we had this big secret."

"Secret?"

"He was teaching me to drive," said Finn.

"We'd go off to a disused industrial estate nearby. And once we were there, he'd let me behind the wheel. Dad knew the owner of the estate, you see. Got his permission. He'd just been through a divorce himself and had a boy the same age as me. Knew what it was like. Knew Dad would do anything for me."

Finn tied a knot in the drawstring.

"And that's the whole point, I guess. Because Dad really *would* do anything for me. He was always there when I needed him. And he listened to what *I* wanted to do. It was special, what we had between us. Really special."

He swallowed.

"But the Sunday before my eleventh birthday – the Sunday before the accident – he told me he couldn't make it the following week. Said he'd see me a different day instead. Said he'd see me the evening of my birthday."

"Why couldn't he make it?"

"He'd been asked to take part in an air display. He'd been invited to co-pilot a reconstructed warplane."

Finn laced a second knot into the drawstring of the anorak.

"And when he told me he couldn't see me, I went ballistic. I shouted at him. Told him he was ratting on our special time. Told him I never wanted to see him again. Told him I hated him."

He pulled the knot tight.

"And those were the last things I ever said to him. We didn't speak all the way home in the car. And then he went out on a practice flight two days later on the morning of my birthday and got himself killed. Ace timing, don't you think?"

Jessie said nothing.

"And I will never, ever forgive myself. Not even if I live to be a hundred."

For a long time neither of them spoke.

And then Jessie turned to him.

"Get up," she said.

Finn stared at her.

"What?"

"I said *get up…*"

Slowly, Finn obeyed.

"Finn Oliver," she said. "You are not a failure. You are nothing of the kind. You said something stupid in the heat of the moment, that's all."

Her eyes burned into his.

"It's time to stop beating yourself up about everything, OK? Time to get your act together and release that Firepearl."

She looked at him slyly.

"Before Morgan gets there first."

Jessie pointed to a series of indents in the rock face not far up from the base.

"There's your first foothold," she said. "And you can grip with your fingers just here."

"Have I got any choice in this?" muttered Finn.

"Not really," said Jessie, her lips twitching. "At least, not if you want to come out of this alive, you haven't."

Finn kicked his right trainer into the rock and lunged towards the finger-holes above his head.

At once he missed the security of his climbing boots. The rounded toe of his trainer felt slippery and clumsy in comparison.

"Now the same thing here," said Jessie. "And here…"

She wafted effortlessly alongside him, indicating more and more tiny pockets in the rock.

"Are you planning on doing this all the way up?" grunted Finn. "I can do this, you know. And I reckon I'd rather find my own route, if that's OK by you."

He heaved himself clear of a patch of loose scree.

"Why don't you go on ahead and tell me what's up there? Give me something to aim for?"

"I'm not going anywhere," returned Jessie. "I'm staying close at hand in case you lose your grip. In case you need me…"

Finn glanced across at her.

"No, Jessie," he said quietly. "I meant what I said,

all right? I have to do this on my own. I have to prove I can do it without my dad."

Jessie hesitated.

She looked back at Finn, her green eyes searching his face.

And then she turned and scorched off in a rapid ascent towards the crest of the rock.

Below her, Finn redoubled his efforts to scale the cliff.

OK, so he'd never climbed solo before.

And he hadn't climbed *at all* since Dad had died.

But Jessie was right.

He had got through fire and water, hadn't he?

And if he could get through those, he could manage this, too.

In any case, he had to be almost halfway up now – and from the top he could hear Jessie shouting down to him.

"I knew it'd be worth it!" she was yelling. "It looks like there's a tiny gap at the top of the dome of flames! I reckon we should be able to see the Inflammati through it… Hang on a second and I'll report back."

Finn paused to catch his breath.

His calf muscles ached and he could taste the salty sweetness of his own blood where he had cut his lip on a sharp snag of rock.

But to get to the summit … to drink in the promised sight of the Inflammati…

It had to be worth it.

It had to be worth every second of it.

He raised his head towards the dome of flame … and the next moment everything seemed to be swimming before his eyes…

His trainers were slipping from their footholds … his fingers were losing their grip … he was sliding … falling…

Finn reached out blindly, his flesh scuffing and tearing against the sharp rock.

For several long seconds he slithered down the face of the cliff, gathering speed as he went.

And then the fingers of his right hand lodged inside a narrow crevice and he jerked to a shaky halt.

His left hand fumbled to join the other, his feet kicked out beneath him…

"Finn! *Finn!* Are you OK?

Jessie was hovering at his side, her voice high and brittle.

"I *told* you I should've stayed with you," she said. "I *told* you, didn't I?"

She reached out towards him.

"Let me help you. Hold you steady for a moment. Show you where to put your hands and feet, at least."

"*Don't … touch … me!*" Finn rasped through

gritted teeth. "Get back up to the top, Jessie. Remember what I said before. I have to do this on my own."

"But—"

"*On my own or not at all.*"

There was a blur of blue as Jessie disappeared from view – and then Finn was alone once more, clinging to the rock, his every muscle taut and trembling.

Somehow he had to find a way to get going again.

Somehow he had to muster the strength to start over.

But even as the thought formed inside his head, he knew that it was no good.

Something inside him had changed.

He couldn't move.

It was as if a force entirely beyond his control had pinned him to the cliff, flattening him against its unforgiving surface.

Of course, he knew the feeling all too well.

He had experienced it many times before.

"Frozen to the rock" Dad had called it – the sensation of being able to move neither up nor down, of being sucked to the cliff like some miserable limpet.

This time, though, it was a million times worse than he had ever known it – this time there was no rope snaking its way up to the summit …

no reassuring harness around him … no voice urging him on from the top…

Or was there something?

Someone seemed to be calling to him … a small, faraway cry coming from somewhere inside his own head…

You can do this, Finn. You can do this if you really want to.

Finn shut his eyes, basking in the warmth of the familiar voice … the familiar words…

Remember what I've always told you. Focus on your breathing – get it so it's nice and steady.

And now he was pushing the air out through pursed lips, willing himself to gain control over his rigid body.

Try to relax, Finn … try to let your body loosen up…

The voice continued to coax him, encourage him, spur him on…

That's better. That's much better. Now find the next foothold. Find a grip for your fingers above you.

Finn opened his eyes – and slowly … shakily … began to move up the rock face.

He passed the point where he had lost his grip just minutes before, concentrating every atom of his energy on the area just ahead of him.

That's it, Finn. That's my boy. You're doing great … just great.

The voice was fading away, retreating inside him – but Finn sensed it was still there somewhere, just within his reach if he needed it again…

And now he was scaling the cliff as if he had done so a thousand times before, as if he had been born purely for this moment.

His breathing was relaxed, his body felt free and fluid, the thrill of adventure coursed like electricity through his veins…

And all at once the summit was upon him – and he was scrambling over the top to the sound of Jessie's cheers and flinging himself to the ground.

Finn lay on his stomach, listening to the wild tattoo of his heart beating against his chest.

Dad would have been proud of him. Really proud. If he'd been there right now he'd have been slapping him on the back and breaking open a slab of chocolate as a reward. They'd have been cracking jokes together, high on the fresh air and the achievement.

And maybe, in some strange but wonderful way, he really was there. Maybe Dad was watching him from above all the time, his very own bright angel – just as Lady Fortescue had said. Maybe he would always be there. Not quite in the way Finn was used to, perhaps. But there all the same. And there just for him.

When at last his pulse had slowed to an even rhythm, Finn rolled himself over on to his back and focused his eyes through the hole in the vast beehive of silvery flames.

But he could see almost nothing.

A mere spatter of pale golden flecks.

A sifting of celestial dust ebbing away into the blackness.

He turned and looked at Jessie.

"I can hardly see them," he said. "It won't be long before they disappear completely."

Jessie nodded.

"I know," she murmured. "I didn't want to tell you earlier. I didn't want to make things worse down there."

She sighed.

"But they're still beautiful, aren't they? Even though they're so weak."

"I've never seen anything so beautiful," whispered Finn. "Not in my whole life."

✳   ✳   ✳

Morgan wheeled round to face Finn and Jessie as they approached the edge of the plateau, his face suffused with disappointment and fury.

"What d'you make of this then?" he snarled, jerking his head towards the Firepearl, which still hovered just the other side of the precipice. "Seems like we've come up against a bit of a problem."

Finn stared suspiciously at the tiny rotating ball of fire.

"You mean you haven't nicked it already, Morgan Bloodaxe?" he said. "What with your criminal record and everything?"

"Think you're so cool, don't you?" sniped back Morgan. "Why don't you try reaching for it yourself, Mortal Boy?"

Finn inched himself towards the edge of the rock and stretched out his hand to touch the Firepearl.

His fingers buckled at once against a wall of solid air.

"It must be the final challenge," he said, frowning. "The challenge of the air. Looks like it's more complicated than a quick smash-and-grab job though, doesn't it? Must've seen you coming a mile off, Morgan."

He looked at Jessie.

"You try it," he said. "It's completely solid. It's as if there's something trapped between us and the Firepearl. It's like…"

He broke off.

"What is it?" said Jessie. "What's the matter?"

"Can't you hear it?"

"Hear what?"

"There's something inside the wall of air," said Finn. "Something vibrating … something moving around…"

He strained his ears against the invisible barrier.

"It's music," he said at last. "I can hear the most incredible music. Surely you can hear it, too?"

Jessie shook her head.

"Can't hear anything," she said. "What kind of music?"

"It's hard to describe," said Finn. "It's kind of *everything*. Every human sound you could possibly imagine all woven together."

Jessie turned to Morgan.

"Hear anything, Bloodaxe?" she snapped.

Morgan narrowed his eyes at her.

"Not a thing, New Girl. Unless you count a couple of imbeciles jabbering away in my ear, that is."

Finn held up his hand.

"Shut up a minute, won't you?" he said. "There's something else … I can hear words inside the wall. Words pushing their way out of all the different sounds."

"He's off his head," muttered Morgan. "Mortal Boy's finally flipped."

But Finn's eyes were shining.

"It's getting clearer now," he said. "It's a question… The music's asking us a question."

Jessie and Morgan stared at him, their faces suddenly alert.

"What is it?" whispered Jessie. "What can you hear?"

Finn listened again.

And as he spoke the words aloud, they seemed to resound through his very soul.

"*What is your greatest wish? …What is your greatest wish? …What is your greatest wish?*"

11.

The Release of the Firepearl

"To take the Firepearl, of course!" cried Morgan, almost before the words were out of Finn's mouth.

He shoved against the wall of air.

"To release it from its enchantments. What other answer could there be? What else could possibly matter?"

And then everything happened at once.

Morgan was catapulted high into the air, his bright figure flung out like a puppet on a string.

Up … up … towards the tiny opening in the dome of enchanted flames.

"*Help me!*" he screamed, but already his voice was no more than a faint echo. "*Help me…*"

Far below him, Finn had fallen to the ground, his hands clamped to his ears.

"What is it, Finn?" cried Jessie.

She bent down and wrenched away his hands.

"*What is it?*"

"It's the music! The music inside the wall of air! It's ripping me apart!"

Jessie's eyes darted up to where Morgan was fast disappearing through the gap in the flames.

Then she stared back at Finn.

"Hold on!" she yelled at him, as he writhed against the screaming of the music. "It'll stop in a moment, Finn. Just hold on!"

And it was just as she said.

As Morgan was blasted clear of the dome of flames and curved away out of sight towards the waters that stormed beneath, Finn's body relaxed at last.

"It's dying away," he said, sitting up again. "It's back to how it was before."

Jessie nodded.

"Yes," she said. "Morgan's gone, hasn't he?"

"You mean…"

"I mean the music was telling you something. Morgan wasn't the right person to answer the question, was he? The Prophecy was true to its word. An immortal could never have released the Firepearl. Not in a million years."

"And you think that's all it was?"

"Of course," said Jessie impatiently. "It was the

right answer, wasn't it? Just not the right person giving it."

She sighed.

"I'm going after him, Finn…"

"*Going after him? But why?*"

"Because he'll be ravaged by the floods in the Gateway otherwise, that's why. I've got to pull him out of the water before it's too late."

"But he tried to get *rid* of you earlier! He tried to force you into the river…"

Jessie shrugged.

"No one deserves to perish in those floodwaters — *no one*. I should know."

"Then I'm coming with you."

"You *can't*, Finn. You've got to stay and finish this off. You've got to do it on your own."

"But—"

"It's the only way … I'm certain it's the only way. Now ask me the question."

"What d'you mean?"

"*Ask me the question … the question inside the music!*"

"You know what the question is."

"*Just ask it!*"

Finn stared at her, open-mouthed.

"Isn't it obvious what I've got to do?" yelled Jessie. "I can't go back through the challenges, can I?

Not without you to hold my hand. I wouldn't get past the flames on my own. *So ask me the question.*"

"But you mustn't do it, Jessie! It's too risky. What if you're thrown into the floodwaters too?"

"I won't be," said Jessie. "I reckon I've got enough energy to cope with anything now. *Ask me the question! Before it's too late…*"

Finn's eyes flashed with fear.

"What … what is your greatest wish?" he cried at last.

"To take the Firepearl!" shouted Jessie, just as Morgan had done only minutes before. "To release it from its enchantments."

A tiny, fragile smile passed between them both.

And then the raucous music filled Finn's head once more and Jessie was pitched upwards towards the gash in the dome of fire – away from Finn … away from the charmed wall of air … away from the Firepearl itself.

"Good luck!" she cried as she vanished out of sight. "It has to be you, Finn! It has to be you!"

✳ ✸ ✳

Morgan hit the rabid floodwaters in precisely the spot his father had perished.

So this was how it had to end.

An action replay of his father's ugly demise.

Already the water had him on his back, devouring him with a greedy thrill.

There was nowhere to gaze but skywards.

And through the mighty fault in the cavern roof Morgan Bloodaxe watched as the Inflammati danced their stately dance of death.

✳   ✳   ✳

"*It has to be you, Finn! It has to be you!*"

Jessie's words resounded in Finn's ears, while the jarring mosaic of music inside the wall of air died away once again to a faint murmur.

So it was down to him after all.

Everything was playing out just as the Prophecy had foretold.

A mortal would release the Firepearl from its elemental enchantments and afford the Fires everlasting protection.

And all that was needed now was for him to answer as the others had done and make a quick grab for the Firepearl.

Nothing more, nothing less.

The Fires … the Underworld … the Inflammati … all saved by a few easy words.

Finn sighed.

Something was nagging away at him.

Maybe, just maybe, being a mortal wasn't going

to be enough on its own.

He bowed his head and listened again for the elusive question.

Had he heard it right?

Had he even heard it at all?

But there it still was, ebbing and flowing amidst the shimmer of music, so close he could almost touch it.

"*What is your greatest wish? ...What is your greatest wish?*"

And without thinking what he was doing or why, Finn raised his pale face once more towards the gap in the dome of flames.

He blinked.

The whole expanse of the heavens was awhirl with dancing stars.

Tiny gold dots of light were darting and shooting across the dark canvas of the sky in a display of celestial fireworks.

And this time they really were blazing.

Incandescent with a dazzling energy.

A final celebration of fiery spirit.

And all at once Finn saw that they were lacing themselves into patterns, engraving the Outer Sphere with loops and chains.

Finn's heart thudded against his chest.

Letters were forming before his very eyes.

Letters and words.

The stars were speaking to him … guiding him…

And only when every point had stilled, only when the airy message of the Inflammati was quite complete, did he dare to read what they had sewn for him across the ebony sky.

"FOLLOW YOUR HEART!" sang the delicate needlework of glittering stars. "FOLLOW YOUR HEART!"

✳   ✳   ✳

The force of the blast was almost too much even for Jessie.

She spun herself clear of the foaming water with less than a second to spare and found herself staring straight into Morgan's disbelieving eyes.

"*Take my hand!*" she screamed.

Morgan opened his mouth to speak but no sound came out.

"*Just take it!*"

Jessie searched the Gateway for a safe haven.

The thick black smoke that had earlier veiled everything in a mantle of secrecy was beginning to lift and below the cliff the Fires were eerily quiet, save for the occasional hiss and splutter.

And still the water kept on pouring in…

Out of the corner of one eye she spotted the narrow shelf on the back wall of the Gateway.

The next minute she was soaring towards it, Morgan's silhouette trailing behind her.

"Why are you doing this?" croaked Morgan, as she laid him down on the shelf. "Why are you helping me? After … after everything I've done?"

Jessie shrugged.

"You're a human being, aren't you? Same as me. Same as everyone else. I was hardly going to leave you to perish."

There was an awkward silence.

"Well, you shouldn't have bothered," said Morgan at last. "I don't need your help, New Girl. I don't need anyone's help, OK? I can look after myself."

He turned the husk of his face away from Jessie.

"Everyone lets you down in the end," he muttered. "You'll see. It's much safer to rely on yourself."

Jessie gaped at him.

"But you can't say that!" she exclaimed. "You've got your dad, haven't you? He hasn't let you down."

Morgan's expression hardened.

"My *father*," he spat, barely able to get the words out, "has let me down worst of all. Worse than you can possibly imagine. And now he's gone for ever. Ravaged by the enchanted flames a few minutes before you and Mortal Boy showed up."

Jessie's eyes bulged.

"And … and your mother? What about her?"

"I never knew my mother. She died when I was born. That's the reason my father hated me so much."

"But she's up there among the Inflammati then, isn't she?" reasoned Jessie. "She's burning away in the Outer Sphere for you to look at whenever you like, Morgan. It's just a different way of being together, that's all."

She glanced anxiously at the enchanted dome of flames.

"And for you she'll be the very brightest star of all."

Morgan grunted.

"I suppose she might be," he said, following her gaze. "At least she might if Mortal Boy's doing his job properly in there. If it's not already too late."

✳   ✳   ✳

Perhaps it had just been an illusion.

Perhaps he had imagined the whole thing.

As swiftly as the words had woven themselves across the sky they had now vanished, leaving nothing but the old sea of drowning stars.

Finn scanned the vast black expanse for a trace of alphabetical magic.

But any clue that the words had ever been there had evaporated … and in their place there was something else.

Something within him, welling up inside and pressing against his throat...

A caged monster that had lurked there far too long and now threatened to tear down its bars and break free.

Finn willed himself to stand fast.

Somehow he must continue to fight it.

After all, he'd had more than enough practice.

He must clench his tongue against his teeth...

Tense every muscle of his aching body...

Concentrate on something else...

Anything else...

He glanced back at the glowing Firepearl.

Just a few simple words and he could surely reach out and claim it for himself.

And then it would all be over.

And yet ... and yet ... if he truly searched his soul – if he followed his fractured heart as the stars had seemed to bid him just moments before, then he knew that the easy answer was not the right answer.

That the capture of the Firepearl was not in fact his greatest wish.

Not quite.

The Fires ... the Underworld ... the Inflammati...

Of course they all mattered.

But something else came first.

Something else definitely came first.

Finn lifted his head.

He was shivering now, cold almost past the point of caring.

The fragile skin under his right eye pulsed and fluttered and his hair clung in matted streaks to his forehead.

"Dad?" he whispered. "Dad? Are you there?"

He sank to his knees.

"I'm sorry, Dad … I'm sorry for everything…"

And already the demon straining at his throat was breaking loose – bursting against his chest, inside his head, behind his eyes…

"I miss you so much," he wept, everything unravelling inside him. "I wish I'd said goodbye… I wish I hadn't said those terrible things. You know I didn't mean them, don't you? I wish … I wish…"

He broke off – and the howl that erupted from him cleaved the wall of solid air apart.

All the music of the universe began to fall away, bowing out to this most ancient of human sounds.

"I wish I'd told you that I loved you…"

And now it was unstoppable, a flood of hot tears springing from his swelling heart and coursing down his cheeks into his open mouth.

A wild tearing of the soul.

A true and terrible release.

And though it might simply have been the

wetness in his eyes, it seemed that above him the Inflammati now shone a little more brightly.

Finn lowered his head at last, his chest still heaving.

He looked out across the thinning wall of air.

And in his tears there were mirrored a thousand Firepearls, a thousand tiny globes of palest red, shimmering in a kaleidoscope of sorrow.

In front of him the music was dying away, the air was freeing.

It had to be now.

Surely it had to be now.

Finn reached out blindly through the dissolving music.

He could sense its closeness now, just a hair's breadth away.

His fingers curled around the radiant Firepearl.

But as he drew back his hand and opened his fist to gaze upon the long-awaited prize, he saw that it was quite empty.

The Firepearl had gone.

It had melted at his touch.

12.

The Birthday
Present

Steam filled every crevice of the Gateway.

Great clouds of it rose from the ground and cleansed the sooty air.

The dome of flames had disappeared and all the protective enchantments with it.

And in their place, hunched in a ball of human misery in the very centre of the great cavern, knelt Finn.

He heard Jessie's voice speak his name, but refused to look up.

"You don't have to tell me," he said flatly, his head in his hands. "I know. I've let everyone down. I've messed up. I didn't answer the question as we'd agreed."

"But Finn—"

"I couldn't, OK, I just couldn't. The Firepearl

wasn't my greatest wish, Jessie. It wasn't what I wanted most of all."

Jessie stared around at the haze of rising steam.

Above them Morgan hung back sulkily on the narrow ledge.

"So what *did* you want most of all?"

Finn's voice came back muffled.

"I wanted to tell my father that I loved him. I wanted to tell him that I was sorry for all the things I said to him that last day we spent together. I wanted to tell him how much I miss him…"

"And that's what you said?"

Finn nodded.

Fresh tears were spilling from his eyes.

"I said it all out loud," he muttered. "And then I kind of lost it … and it felt … oh, Jessie … it felt like the best thing in the world. It felt as if all the hurt was being taken away. But then when I reached out to take the Firepearl, it dissolved in my hand. I didn't release the Firepearl, Jessie. Do you hear what I'm saying? After everything we've been through, I didn't release the Firepearl."

Jessie bent down and eased his hands from his pale face.

"But you did, Finn," she said, brushing away his tears. "It's exactly what you did. How else could I be here with you now? Look up… Look around you.

Look at what you've done."

And slowly, Finn raised his head.

Around him every last drop of water had evaporated.

Below the cliff at the far end of the Gateway, the Fires roared in celebration.

And above him, through the jagged fault in the rock, the golden Inflammati blazed.

"But how…?"

"By telling the truth, Finn. That's how. You told the truth to yourself. You let yourself cry for your father. And each and every one of those tears was the true Firepearl. The other pearl was just an illusion. Don't you see, Finn? By saving yourself, you have saved everything."

Finn opened his mouth to speak.

But before he could say a word, a noise like the rushing wind rose up from outside the Gateway.

And down the steps swooped thousands upon thousands of whirling spirits, each one bursting with light and colour.

"Just look at them all!" cried Jessie. "They're brighter than I've ever seen them. And Morgan too, up there on the ledge. Back to his full spirit form. Probably psyching himself up to cause a bit more trouble…"

Edric swished through the dazzling throng and landed at Finn's feet.

"It's too bad I won't be able to see them once I'm back on the Other Side."

Jessie followed Finn's gaze.

"Mr Glenridding says he's never seen them shine so brilliantly," she said. "And your dad will always be there, Finn. He'll be watching over you for ever."

Finn nodded.

"I know," he said. "But it won't be quite the same, will it?"

Jessie's face clouded over.

"Nothing's going to be the same," she said. "Not when you've gone back. I'm going to miss you so much. You've been like a real brother to me."

"You've been pretty fantastic yourself," mumbled Finn. "I couldn't have done any of this without you."

He glanced up at the narrow shelf where Morgan still sat scowling down at the maelstrom of partying ghosts.

"Look on the bright side, Jessie," he said, suppressing a laugh. "You've got Morgan for company now."

Jessie grunted.

"Oh great," she replied. "That *so* cheers me up. Morgan Bloodaxe has a few nasty habits to kick before he gets to hang out with me, I can tell you."

Glenridding and Lady Fortescue hovered towards

them in a cocktail of burgundy doublet and green skirts.

"Care to join us?" cried Glenridding's voice from somewhere inside the amorous blend of spirits. "Thought we'd start a grand procession around the Gateway. Wondered whether you'd do us the honour of leading it, Master Oliver?"

"I'd love to," said Finn. "But then I want to get back to the Other Side, if that's OK with you. I'd like to spend the last few minutes of my birthday with my mum. I reckon I owe her."

"Not a problem," replied Glenridding. "I'll escort you to the upper passageways just as soon as you're ready. It will be my pleasure."

He beamed at Lady Fortescue.

"Funny to think of Master Oliver getting out that way, isn't it? No fancy Exit Ascents for him."

Beside them, Finn's face had suddenly lit up.

"Of *course*!" he exclaimed. "Why didn't I think of it before?"

He turned to Glenridding.

"I need a private word with Jessie," he said. "I'll be over in just a second."

"What is it?" asked Jessie, as Glenridding and Lady Fortescue glided discreetly to one side.

"I've thought of a way we can still see each other," said Finn triumphantly. "If you can wangle a few extra Exit Ascents, then I'll meet you outside The Rose and Eagle on Saturday afternoons."

"You'll *what*?"

"I'll meet you outside The Rose and Eagle. You know, my aunt's pub – the one I was telling you about. Dead simple for you to get to. In the warm weather she lets me sit in the beer garden. Otherwise I just hang out in the back room with the pool table and the darts and things. Family privilege. We could have a laugh together."

"But would I be allowed in?"

"Don't see why not," said Finn. "You're family too, after all. Not that I'd tell anyone that. Might be a bit hard to explain. And it'd probably be a good idea to hide that locket of yours… But seriously, no one'll ask any questions. They'll just be glad I've got some company for once. And we can always go off for a walk together if you feel really awkward."

Jessie considered for a moment.

"I suppose I'd be fulfilling my duties," she said. "Looking out for my descendants and everything."

She grinned at Finn.

"OK, then," she said. "You've got yourself a deal. I'll be outside The Rose and Eagle every Saturday at half past three. Starting this weekend. If I can twist Mr Glenridding's arm, that is."

"He'll be a pushover," said Finn.

"And don't forget what Edric told you either," Jessie reminded him. "You've got a fragment of the immortal in you now, Finn. You can come back to the Underworld whenever you like."

Finn pulled a face.

"I'll have to think about that one," he said. "Reckon I could do with a rest right now. But one thing's for sure…"

"What's that?" asked Jessie.

"If I do ever come back, I'll be taking it nice and easy through the upper passageways. I'm done with short cuts. There'll be no more falling down Exit 43 for me!"

*   *   *

Finn lowered the cold slab of stone back on to the empty grave and glanced around him.

The storm had cleared away completely and a bright moon illuminated the graveyard.

His heart leaped into his mouth as a cat sprang out from the shadows.

He clicked his tongue in annoyance.

Nearly two days in the company of the Woken Dead and all it took was a stupid cat to freak him out now he was back on the Other Side.

Not very impressive.

Definitely time to get home and sort things

out with Mum.

He was partway to the lychgate when he stopped short.

It was the strong scent of damp moss that made him turn back.

Just behind him stood an old Victorian headstone.

A perfectly ordinary Victorian headstone.

Except for one thing.

The long wet grass by the side of the grave had been trampled quite flat and the moss had only very recently been picked off the stone to reveal the inscription.

Finn bent down to read it.

IN LOVING MEMORY OF JESSICA EMILY SHERRATT

BELOVED DAUGHTER AND SISTER

1848-1859

Something halfway between a shiver of pleasure and fear coursed down his spine.

He ran his finger over the rough stone.

"See you, Jessie," he murmured.

And then he turned on his heel and headed for home.

When his mother opened the door to him, she pulled him into her arms and hugged him as if she would never let him go.

"Finn!" she sobbed. "Oh, Finn! You've come back! I've been sick with worry... What with the police not finding any trace of the car and—"

"I can explain about the car," muttered Finn. "Or at least, I can try to. You see—"

His mother held him even tighter.

"Not now," she said. "It doesn't matter. We can talk about all that tomorrow. Nothing matters to me right now except that I've got you home."

She pulled away at last.

"Happy birthday, sweetheart," she said, holding him gently by the shoulders. "Things are going to be different this year. Very different. I want to be there for you, Finn. None of this lounging around in bed all day like a wet weekend. It's back to being a proper mum again for me."

She ruffled his hair.

"And that starts right now with packing you off to bed. You look like you haven't slept in weeks."

Finn glanced past her into the house.

"There's something I've got to do first," he said. "Something I should've done this time last year. You – you can come and watch me if you want."

He led the way upstairs to his bedroom and went over to the dresser.

His mother watched in silence as he bent down and opened the bottom drawer.

"You know what this is, don't you?" he said, pulling out a large package.

She nodded, her eyes bright with tears.

Finn carried the parcel carefully over to his bed and sat down.

"Sorry," he said, looking down at his fuzzy reflection in the shiny gold wrapping-paper. "I just couldn't bear to touch it before. It's been sitting in that drawer a whole year, Mum ... a whole year."

Slowly, he began to peel off the tape.

"Feels really weird – knowing Dad was the last to see inside this paper."

The final strip of tape came away and Finn eased open the parcel.

For a moment he simply stared at its contents.

"You do like it?" said his mother anxiously, perching beside him on the bed.

Finn swallowed.

"*Like it?*" he said. "It's the very best present he could ever have given me."

"Well, that's all right, then. I was in on it too, you see. Dad told me you'd been doing a bit of star-gazing together after that school trip to the London Planetarium. And we put our heads together and came up with the idea of a telescope."

"Put your *heads* together? But I thought you weren't even *talking* to each other?"

His mother sighed.

"Of course we were talking to each other, Finn. I never stopped loving your father, you know. Just couldn't live with him, that's all."

Finn glanced at her.

"Because of all the flying and stuff? Because he was such a daredevil? Was that what you couldn't deal with?"

"That was part of it, I suppose," said his mother. "He certainly liked his risks. But it was just how he was. He had to follow his heart. Like all of us have to."

"I know," said Finn. "I know that now."

His mother put her arm around him.

"Perhaps we could set up the telescope together tomorrow evening," she said. "If we get another nice clear night like this one's turned out to be."

"I'd like that," said Finn.

He stood up and padded over to the window.

"When did all the rain stop?" he asked.

"Cleared up very suddenly a couple of hours ago," said his mother. "Around ten o'clock, I suppose. Surely you must've noticed? Went from storm-force ten to a beautiful April night in a matter of seconds. Almost spooky."

Finn smiled to himself and looked up at the night sky.

There they all were.

Orion's Belt. The Plough. The Great Bear.

The usual suspects.

Every one of them in their rightful position.

And then he looked again.

There was something else.

Something new and yet completely familiar, pulsing into life over to the west.

He opened the window wide.

"Mum?" he said, leaning out. "Come over here… Tell me what you can see… Above the moor…"

His mother joined him at the window.

"Just a beautifully clear night sky," she said. "Just…"

She broke off.

"I – I can see a million golden stars," she whispered. "A million tiny golden stars…"

Finn nodded.

"Thought so," he said. "Just making sure."

He knelt at the open window and gazed out through the cool night at the glister of dancing stars.

And it seemed to him that one shone more brightly than any other.

✳